"What makes you think my comment was innocent, Sara?"

"Well, because Max, I'm sure you've never thought of me in that way."

She couldn't see all his features clearly, but she could see his mouth. The lower lip was slightly fuller than the upper, which was bowed in the middle, enough to make it sensuous, not enough to make him appear any less masculine.

"Does that mean you've never thought of me like that?"

"Yes."

He brushed her cheek, only the pads of his fingers touching her, but her whole body felt the contact. "So it hadn't occurred to you that the reason I agreed to look for Larry was because *you* asked me to?"

Her throat felt so thick she could barely answer. "No."

"And you don't think that I want to kiss you now?"

She shook her head.

"Then you'd be wrong," he whispered.

D1565329

Dear Reader,

If you asked my father if he were an American hero, he'd say no. Yet he won a Bronze Star for bravery during World War II and sacrificed three years of his twenties in a North Korean prison camp because of his fervent belief in democracy.

More impressive, he's a good man who loves his family even more than his country and always tries to do the right thing. I think he's all the more extraordinary because he doesn't know that he is.

Like my father, Max Dolinger doesn't realize he's a hero. A cop turned FBI agent, Max has long been trying to pay back society for the sins of his parents. Along the way he's not only turned into the best of men but fallen for a friend's girl he's honor bound not to touch.

But now his friend and the woman he's already half in love with are no longer together, and all bets are off. Can this good man get what he deserves: the love of a good woman?

All my best,

Darlene Gardner

P.S. Online readers can visit me at www.darlenegardner.com.

Books by Darlene Gardner

DARLENE GARDNER

TO THE MAX

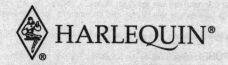

HARLEQUIN®

TORONTO • NEW YORK • LONDON
AMSTERDAM • PARIS • SYDNEY • HAMBURG
STOCKHOLM • ATHENS • TOKYO • MILAN • MADRID
PRAGUE • WARSAW • BUDAPEST • AUCKLAND

If you purchased this book without a cover you should be aware
that this book is stolen property. It was reported as "unsold and
destroyed" to the publisher, and neither the author nor the
publisher has received any payment for this "stripped book."

To my father, Charles Hrobak,
because he's always been my hero.

ISBN 0-373-69219-6

TO THE MAX

Copyright © 2005 by Darlene Hrobak Gardner.

All rights reserved. Except for use in any review, the reproduction or
utilization of this work in whole or in part in any form by any electronic,
mechanical or other means, now known or hereafter invented, including
xerography, photocopying and recording, or in any information storage
or retrieval system, is forbidden without the written permission of the
publisher, Harlequin Enterprises Limited, 225 Duncan Mill Road,
Don Mills, Ontario, Canada M3B 3K9.

All characters in this book have no existence outside the imagination of
the author and have no relation whatsoever to anyone bearing the same
name or names. They are not even distantly inspired by any individual
known or unknown to the author, and all incidents are pure invention.

This edition published by arrangement with Harlequin Books S.A.

® and TM are trademarks of the publisher. Trademarks indicated with
® are registered in the United States Patent and Trademark Office, the
Canadian Trade Marks Office and in other countries.

www.eHarlequin.com

Printed in U.S.A.

1

THE LAST TIME Max Dolinger indulged himself with a long look at Sara Reynolds, he'd been at a wedding and a guy he'd known since grade school had threatened to flatten his nose.

If the guy hadn't been well on his way to getting smashed at the open bar paid for by the groom's parents, he would have realized two things:

He didn't have a fighting chance against Max, who was bigger, taller and trained to defend himself. And Max would never make a move on a friend's girl, even if the friend wasn't much of a friend and the girl was very much a woman.

Max looked his fill at Sara now, very much doubting anything or anybody could have made him look away.

He'd been in the backyard returning his late grandfather's ancient lawn mower to the shed when he'd heard a car rumble up the long gravel driveway. When he'd come to check it out, he'd seen Sara breezing up the sidewalk back into his life.

Appropriately, a storm was brewing. The wind swept up and over the rise. It rustled the leaves of the tall oak trees and bushy sweet gums in the front yard that were just starting to show their fall colors and blew strands of honey-blond hair into Sara's face.

Late September in Maryland could still be hot, and today was unseasonably warm. Sara's sundress was appropriate for the temperature, but not for the wind. When she let go of the skirt to brush back her hair, the wind lifted the gauzy material and bared her shapely legs.

For scintillating seconds, she reminded him of that famous pose of Marilyn Monroe with her skirt billowing as she straddled a New York subway grate. Sara's figure wasn't quite as lush as the movie star's and her white panties were dotted with red polka dots, but Sara wasn't posing. Max thought that made her look even sexier than Marilyn had.

But what was Sara Reynolds doing here?

Nobody except a couple of friends and the real-estate agent who'd spent the past eighteen months hounding him to sell his late grandparents' spread knew he was back in rural Maryland.

He doubted the FBI field office in El Paso leaked information on where special agents spent their vacations, though he couldn't imagine why Sara would ask.

He'd only seen her twice before, and that had been shortly before he'd left Maryland for the FBI. A buddy from high school had gotten married and invited the old crowd, which included both Max and Larry Brunell, to his wedding. Larry, the punch-drunk guy, had shown up with Sara.

Max had noticed her at the rehearsal dinner even before she'd beaten him to the mother of the bride, who'd been choking on a piece of filet mignon. After performing the Heimlich, she'd stroked the older woman's arm and deflected her embarrassment with a funny story about how she'd tripped on the wedding runner and crashed into the best man the last time she'd been a bridesmaid.

Max had fallen a little in love at that moment. At the wedding the next afternoon, he couldn't help but notice Sara looking like a vision in a creamy backless gown, her honey-blond hair swept off her neck.

Unfortunately, Larry had noticed him noticing and asked why Max was staring at his girl. It hadn't occurred to Max to tell anything but the truth.

"Because she's gorgeous."

That had set off the fireworks, not that anyone had seen them flare except Larry and Max. The irony of it was that Max had merely talked to Sara. Out of consideration for Larry, he hadn't even asked her to dance.

"Stay the hell away from her," Larry had sneered.

Max had stayed away, not because he was afraid of Larry but because he feared the scene Larry might make at their buddy's wedding.

Max hadn't seen Sara since then. Until now.

And now he was getting an eyeful.

She wrestled the material of her skirt back in place and held it awkwardly around her legs. Shuffling up the sidewalk, she climbed the wooden porch steps he'd repaired the previous morning and knocked on the heavy oak door.

Figuring there was only one sure way to find out why she was here, he emerged from the shadow his grandparents' sprawling house cast on the just-mowed lawn. Stepping into the sliver of sunshine the overhead clouds hadn't yet obliterated, he opened his mouth to announce his presence.

"Hello, Max." Sara started talking before he did, except her eyes were on the door instead of him. "I hope you remember who I am, because you sure made an impression on me."

She made a purely female noise of approval that reminded him of a cat's purr. "Not a bad opening but not quite right."

Max frowned and forgot about announcing himself.

"I should get straight to the point. Yeah, that's it. I'll blurt it right out." She lowered her voice. "I want you, Max."

His heart gave a bounce worthy of one of those synthetic rubber balls with the super spring. Had that strong current of attraction he'd experienced at the wedding flowed both ways?

"No," she said. "That's all wrong, too. How about, I need you, Max."

Could she be talking about… No. It wasn't possible. The way Larry had spun it, he and Sara were headed for happily ever after.

But Max hadn't been back to Maryland since he'd left for his training at the FBI Academy in Quantico a week after the wedding. That had been a full year ago.

She rapped on the door again, harder this time, then heaved a sigh he heard clearly from where he stood.

"What will I do if he doesn't answer the door?" she asked aloud.

"You could turn around and say hello."

She gasped and whirled, her hand flying to her throat. The breeze lifted the skirt of her buttery-yellow sundress, although—damn it—not as high this time. She plastered it down to her side.

With wide brown eyes set in a round face, she was every bit as appealing as the first time he'd seen her.

He liked that she didn't color her fair hair, even though she was neither a blonde nor a brunette but somewhere in between. He liked that she hadn't dieted away her curves. He even liked the way she'd blushed when her skirt flew up.

"Max. I didn't see you."

"If you ask a question, you should expect an answer." He gazed up at her, glad his dark sunglasses hid the hope that surely burned in his eyes.

He'd put her out of his mind a long time ago, but the thought of her still cropped up at unexpected moments. He'd caught her watching him a couple times at the wedding but hadn't considered that she'd given him a second thought. He considered it now.

"I was talking to myself," she said. "Usually I know when I'm about to answer back."

A corner of his mouth quirked and his mood lightened. A few minutes ago, when he'd pushed the lawn mower over grass that neither of his grandparents would ever step on again, he'd have thought that impossible. "Hello, Sara."

"You do remember who I am then? I was afraid when I was driving over here that you wouldn't."

"A woman who can perform the Heimlich is a hard woman to forget," he said. An understatement.

She descended the porch steps and offered him the hand that wasn't holding her skirt in place. It was small, warm and in his grasp far too briefly.

Her eyes flickered to his, then away. She took a giant step backward, and he started to think he'd misinterpreted what he'd overheard.

"How have you been, Max? When I talked to you at Kevin Carmichael's wedding, you were about to enter the FBI. I understand you're stationed in Texas. How's that working out for you?"

"It's working out fine," he said slowly, "but I get the feeling you didn't drive over here to ask me how things were going at the FBI."

"You're right. I didn't." She shifted her weight from one foot to another. She wore sandals, and her toenails, like her fingernails, were painted pink. "You're probably wondering how I knew you were here."

That hadn't been uppermost in his mind. Not after his body had gone on red-hot alert when she'd said she needed him. His groin tightened, but his brain duly registered that she'd shaken his hand. Not exactly standard operating procedure for a woman on the make.

"I called Kevin last night, and his wife said he was out having a drink with you." She indicated the four cardboard boxes on the porch stuffed with useable items earmarked for charity. Even though Max had stayed up half the night filling the boxes after meeting Kevin, he'd barely made a dent in the workload. "You're in town to go through your grandparents' things, aren't you? That must be tough."

Her empathy triggered a wave of sadness. He fought it, consoling himself that both his grandparents had lived long, commendable lives. His grandmother had been a tireless volunteer, and his grandfather a physician who'd served under General Douglas MacArthur in World War II.

"It's got to be done," he said. "The house has been standing empty since my grandmother died, and that was eighteen months ago. It's past time I got the place ready to sell."

"It's a beautiful place." Her eyes roamed over the wraparound porch and bay windows at the front of the two-story, gabled-roof house, which was a soft yellow hue. "That's why I remembered it. Well, sort of remembered. I drove around for what seemed like an hour looking for it. I noticed the house once when Larry took me for a drive to see where he'd grown up, and he mentioned you'd lived here with your grandparents."

Larry. Ah, yes, Larry. How could he have forgotten Larry?

"How is Larry?" he choked out the very question he'd avoided last night when he'd gotten together with Kevin.

"See. Now that's the thing. I'm not sure how Larry is."

He digested that for a moment but couldn't get it to compute. "But it seems to me I heard you two moved in together."

"We did. But he moved out a couple months ago."

"I hadn't heard that," Max said neutrally. He'd been a police detective before an FBI agent. He, better than anyone, knew how to conceal his thoughts.

With any luck, she'd seen through Larry's charming facade the same way Max eventually had. He'd once loved Larry like a brother but had gradually come to realize he was an underachiever, a screwup and one of the most self-involved people Max had ever known.

Sara's eyes met his. He saw need in them, all right. But not the kind running through Max like a hot stream of lava.

"Actually, Larry is the reason I came to see you. I mean, with the two of you being friends and all."

He stiffened. He should have known this was about Larry. At the very least, he shouldn't have deluded himself that he'd made the same kind of impression on Sara that long-ago wedding weekend as she had on him. Overhead, a cloud blotted out the last of the sun.

"I need you…" she began, and for an instant he thought, hoped, he was wrong. But then she finished the sentence, "…to find Larry. He's missing."

THAT HAD BEEN HARD for Sara to say. Others typically came to her for help, not the other way around. She liked to handle her own problems, but too much was at stake to assume she could handle this one.

The wind whipped her hair into her eyes. She brushed it back with the hand not holding her skirt so she could see how her declaration had gone over.

"Have you called the cops?" Max asked, and Sara got her first inkling that this conversation might not go her way.

The man was an FBI agent, for pity's sake. He'd been a Baltimore City cop. Of course he'd try to direct her to the police. She sucked in a deep breath and inhaled the scent of freshly mowed grass and air heavy with the threat of rain.

"This isn't a cop kind of thing," she hedged.

"Last I checked, cops found missing persons."

"I know that." She considered how to put the best possible spin on her story. "But Larry isn't *missing* missing."

He didn't say anything, but stood there in the

gathering gloom looking imposing. Six feet something of well-muscled male. He was the same age as Larry, which made him thirty or thereabouts.

Somebody at the wedding had told her that Max was part Cuban but she'd guessed at his Hispanic heritage before then. It was there in his well-defined cheekbones, skin that appeared perpetually sun-burnished, black hair and eyes she knew were brown beneath his dark sunglasses.

He wore a sleeveless white T-shirt and athletic shorts that displayed so much skin it was almost visual overkill. He wasn't as bulked up as a bodybuilder but he definitely logged gym time. The deltoid muscles in his shoulders alone were to swoon for.

She'd been intrigued by him at the wedding but only partly because of his good looks. He'd been called upon to tie the groom's tie, deliver the toast, deal with a groomsman who'd had too much to drink and a half-dozen other small things.

Sara had been left with the impression of a man his friends could rely on.

She plunged ahead. "I mean Larry isn't missing like those poor people you sometimes hear about whose cars are found abandoned or whose houses are left trashed. Larry is just, well, gone."

More silence, if you didn't count the howling of the mischievous wind. It kicked up a swirl of dirt and grass that stung her lower legs.

Damn those dark sunglasses, which the clouds had made superfluous anyway. They hid his eyes and whatever he was thinking. Not that she had much hope of figuring out what went on in that dark, handsome head of his anyway.

She suspected he and Larry weren't the closest of friends, but they'd kept in at least casual touch since high school. Add the fact that Max was an FBI agent and had been a cop. When she'd heard he was in town, coming to him had seemed like a no-brainer.

"You probably want details," she said. "What? When? Where? How? That kind of thing."

He nodded toward the front door. "You'd better come in."

She started up wooden steps that seemed as though they'd recently been repaired. The steps led to the house that had stuck in her memory, complete with details such as the hanging swing on the wide porch and the fancy scrollwork on the porch trim.

She stumbled slightly and reached for the handrail, releasing her dress in the process. The wind took that moment to deliver another skirt-tenting blow. She clutched at the material again but not until it had already taken to the air.

She cursed her decision to wear the sundress. The threat of rain had made the weather hot and sticky and she'd wanted to look her best when she came to see him, but jeans and a tank top were more her style.

Turning to make sure Max hadn't gotten an eyeful, she saw that his sunglasses were trained squarely on her butt.

"Sorry," she mumbled.

His chin lifted so the sunglasses pointed at her face. "Don't apologize. I like polka dots."

She whirled back around, remembering she'd

pulled on white bikini panties with red polka dots that morning. She fielded much more suggestive compliments at the pub where she worked, but this one affected her to her toes.

"Keep going and you'll run into the kitchen." Max's voice came from behind her. She kept walking, warning herself not to read anything into his comment.

He'd paid little notice to her last year, even taking into consideration she'd been his friend's girl at the time. He wouldn't be dealing with her now if she hadn't shown up on his doorstep.

She resolved to pretend he'd never commented on her underwear. She needed to sit down at the scarred wooden table in the cheerful country kitchen and get down to the business of enlisting his help.

That's why she'd come here, after all.

"Would you like something to drink?" He moved past her into the heart of the kitchen and opened the refrigerator door. "I don't drink soda but I have bottled water."

She wondered if he were a health nut partial to fruit, grains and vegetables and went with the flow.

"Water's fine," she said at the same moment she noticed the half-eaten box of chocolate-chip cookies on the counter behind her. She hid a smile, liking knowing that the big, tough, ripped FBI agent had a sweet tooth.

He uncapped both bottles of water, then handed one to her. He'd taken off his sunglasses and his dark eyes focused on her. Her stomach did a dip worthy of a roller-coaster plunge.

He had beautiful eyes, thickly lashed and so dark they appeared almost black. The color lent them an intensity that sent anticipation rushing through her. Her heart thudded, her lips parted and she held her breath.

"You've got a leaf in your hair."

She swiped at her hair, feeling foolish and out of sorts because of it.

"Other side." He reached across the counter separating them, and her pulse raced as his fingers grazed her scalp and he plucked out the leaf.

When he straightened from the counter to deposit the leaf in the kitchen trash can, she needed a moment to regain her equilibrium.

He was just a man like any other, she told herself firmly. And she was the woman who needed his help.

She sat down at the well-worn, square table and watched as Max lowered himself into the slat-backed chair across from her.

In the confines of the kitchen, he seemed somehow bigger, the muscles in his arms even more impressive. His thick hair was slightly damp where it met his brow, and he smelled earthy and masculine, an exhilarating combination. He tipped back the water bottle, and the long, tanned column of his throat worked as he swallowed.

Sara swallowed, too.

Max's dark eyes locked on hers when he put down the bottle of water, and she realized he was watching her studying him. Check that. *Staring* at him.

"If you don't mind my saying," he said, "you don't seem too concerned about Larry."

His observation jolted her back to her mission. Even though she found Max undeniably attractive, she hadn't come here to indulge herself. As though she ever did that anyway.

"I'm not concerned about Larry," she said, then realized how cold that sounded. "I mean, I am and I'm not. I need to find him but I don't think anything terrible has happened to him."

"I don't understand."

"You know Larry bartends at the Rusty Nail Pub, right?"

He nodded.

"I'm a waitress there. He called work a few days ago to say he needed to take some time off but didn't say where he was going or when he'd be back."

"That's not what I meant." Max leaned back in his seat, the lazy pose making him look even sexier. "I don't understand why you need to find him."

Sara rubbed her forehead, because they'd finally arrived at the crux of the problem. The calendar hanging from the kitchen wall wasn't current, but she was well aware that today was Saturday.

"If I don't find Larry by Friday," she said, "Johnny could go to jail."

2

WHO IN THE HELL was Johnny?

Max had been bracing himself to hear that Sara had realized her life wasn't complete without Larry when she'd thrown another man into the mix.

Not only that, the man sounded like bad news. In Max's considerable law-enforcement experience, good guys had no reason to steer clear of the cops. The overwhelming majority of the time, somebody afraid of landing in jail belonged there.

And now Sara had gotten herself involved with one of these jokers, who was somehow mixed up with Larry.

Although a dozen other questions would have been more relevant, he found himself asking, "Does Johnny live with you?"

Sara nodded. "He moved in when Larry moved out."

If jealousy were a color, Max's world would have turned green. He didn't like that this man, who by all indications had criminal tendencies, had been Johnny-on-the-spot when Larry moved out.

"It didn't take you long to replace Larry." Max tried his best not to sound surly but doubted he managed it.

"I needed to. I had trouble making rent even before I started nursing school. Now that I'm going to Johns Hopkins, it's even tougher. And, besides, Johnny really needed a place to stay."

At any other time, Max would have been impressed. He'd lived in Baltimore long enough to be aware of the nursing school's reputation as one of the finest in the nation.

Not only that, the nursing profession seemed to suit Sara. Hell, hadn't she been the one to perform the Heimlich at the wedding last year?

But Max couldn't bring himself to congratulate her for being accepted into Johns Hopkins. Not when Johnny loomed on the horizon. "What does Johnny do?"

"He's working the counter at a coffee shop while studying to get his GED."

Max's impression of Johnny deteriorated even further. The man Sara had described, although trying to better himself, sounded more like a burden than a help. "I'm surprised he can afford to pay half the rent."

"He can't. He only pays about a third. I work an extra shift at Rusty's whenever I can to make up for the rest."

Max squashed his urge to point out she was flanked by men who weren't good for her: Johnny at home, and Larry at work. He phrased his next question as diplomatically as he could. "It doesn't bother you that Johnny doesn't pull his weight?"

Sara shrugged. "Not really. Johnny's eighteen. If I hadn't said he could stay with me, he'd probably still be living in the retirement community in Sarasota with our parents. And that's not the place for him."

"Johnny's your brother?" he guessed, as though saying it aloud would help that fact sink in.

"My only brother," she answered, and the righteous anger that had pumped up Max's body seeped away. "My only sibling period. Maybe that's why I worry about him so much."

Now that Max knew Johnny and Sara were related, it changed things. But it didn't change everything. That not-so-minor matter of Johnny and jail remained. "It sounds like Johnny's given you something to worry about."

She reached across the table and covered his hand. Hers felt small and smooth and warm. Their eyes locked, and again he felt that charged current flow between them. But then she broke the contact, and he wondered if he'd imagined it because he wanted it to be there.

"I didn't mean to give you the impression that Johnny was a criminal or anything like that," she said, tucking her hands out of sight under the table. "He's a good kid who made a bad decision."

Max had heard variations of that one before. As an excuse, it ranked right up there with *he was at the wrong place at the wrong time* and *he's a good kid who got mixed up with a bad crowd*. Nobody ever admitted their relative was the bad in the crowd.

"You better start at the beginning," Max said.

"Okay." Sara pursed her full, ripe lips and tapped them with a knuckle. "For as long as I can remember, Johnny's had this baseball with Babe Ruth's signature on it."

Before Max could become impressed, his natural skepticism kicked in. "Is the autograph genuine?"

"That's the thing. We never thought so. My dad found the ball in his dad's attic. Years ago an authenticator told him it was a fake. So he gave it to Johnny, who was always trying to impress his friends. When Johnny showed the ball to Larry, I gather Larry was impressed."

"You gather? You weren't there when this happened?"

She shook her head. "No. Johnny and Larry, they're friends. I'm telling you the story the way Johnny told me."

"Go on."

"Larry said that maybe the authenticator had been wrong. He said he knew a collector who could take another look at it. He proposed he and Johnny split the profits fifty-fifty if the collector bought the ball."

"Sounds like a pretty steep cut to me."

"Johnny didn't think so. Remember, he was pretty sure the ball was worthless. So he said sure, why not? To make a long story short, the guy offered to buy. Apparently he was so anxious to have the ball that he went to the bank and had a cashier's check cut."

Max rubbed his chin but said nothing. Savvy sellers knew that unhappy buyers could put a stop payment on a personal check. The average cashier's check didn't come with the option to change your mind.

"How much did they get for the ball?"

"Fifteen thousand dollars."

Max whistled. The amount sounded high even if the ball were in mint condition and the autograph genuine. Sara's hand reappeared and shoved through her hair. She didn't look happy.

"This story doesn't have a happy ending, does it?" he asked, and she shook her head.

"A few days ago, the man came into the Coffee Ground—that's the shop where Johnny works. He said he tried to get the ball authenticated and found out it was a fake." Sara paused, blew out a breath, rubbed the back of her neck. "He wants his money back."

"So why didn't Johnny give it to him?"

"He only had half of it. Larry has the rest."

"So Larry split with the money when he found out the guy wanted it back?"

"Not according to my brother," Sara said. "The man bought the baseball on Wednesday but didn't come to the coffee shop until Friday. Larry left on Thursday."

"Convenient timing."

Sara ignored his comment. "The bottom line is the man would rather have his money back than press charges. But he said he'd file a complaint with the police unless he has every cent by Friday. That's why I need to find Larry. Unless he comes back and straightens this out, Johnny's going to get caught in the crossfire."

Max stifled a sigh, having a hard time drumming up sympathy for Johnny or Larry. "Do you really believe either of them thought that autograph was genuine?"

Sara's brown eyes flashed, shooting off sparks. "I think both of them wanted to believe Babe Ruth signed that ball. Wouldn't you?"

"Well, yeah, but I wouldn't sell it to somebody unless I was sure."

"I already told you. They thought the buyer was an expert."

"Apparently he wasn't. Which brings up another question. If he wasn't an expert, why would he buy the ball without having it authenticated first?"

"I don't know," Sara said.

Max studied her, but he read hope on her face rather than conviction. She wanted to believe her brother hadn't deliberately conned a man into buying a worthless baseball.

Max didn't know what her brother was capable of but he could easily believe the worst of Larry.

He'd always be grateful to Larry for befriending him when he first moved to Maryland, but he'd hung out with him less and less as the years passed.

Still he'd heard stories about Larry sneaking in the back door of the movie theater, jumping the fence at a high school football game to avoid paying admission and slipping candy into his pockets at the convenience store.

"Let me ask you something." He tried to think of a way to be tactful, but couldn't come up with one. "Why are you letting their problem become your problem?"

"Because Johnny's my brother! He needs me."

He wondered for a fleeting moment what it would be like to have Sara standing fiercely by his side, depressed by the thought that he'd probably never find out.

"I can respect that. I even admire it. But your brother needs to take some responsibility." Max indicated the room with a sweep of his hand. "Where is he? Why didn't he come with you?"

"He had to work this morning, then he was going to the library to study."

"Leaving you to clean up his mess," Max finished.

She got up and paced to the far end of the kitchen before returning to the table. She was average height, five feet six at the most. But the indignation she didn't try to disguise seemed to fill her up, making her appear taller. "Leaving me to ask for help from an FBI agent who happens to be a friend of the missing person we need to find."

"A missing person who might have deliberately disappeared with money he and Johnny got in a con." Max set his jaw. "You want to know what I think? I think you should call the police and let them handle this."

SARA STARED DUMBFOUNDED at Max, angry at herself for getting distracted by his biceps and triceps and deltoids. The man had dared advocate getting the cops involved when she'd been desperately trying to avoid exactly that.

Yes, he was an FBI agent so it stood to reason he had a strong sense of right and wrong. But she'd pegged him as a man who'd be willing to go the distance for his friends.

Because he'd known Larry since childhood, she'd hoped he'd overlook the vague sense of unease about the sale of the baseball that even she couldn't escape.

She wasn't asking him to break the law. She was asking him to find his friend and in the process stop the law from sucking Johnny into the legal system. Again.

Sara had intended to be completely up front with Max about Johnny's juvenile record, but now she didn't dare risk revealing the entire reason she didn't want the police involved. But she had to say something persuasive. Right now.

"What if I get my brother on the phone and let him tell you the story? Surely I've left out a few things he could explain better."

From the set of Max's mouth, it seemed as though he might refuse outright but then he sighed. "Fine. Use the phone on the wall. I'll listen to what he has to say."

Sara picked up the receiver, quickly dialed Johnny's cell phone, then felt her palms grow damp as she listened to the shrill rings at the other end of the line. After six of them, the voice mail kicked in.

"He must be somewhere he can't get service," she said after leaving a message. "Or maybe he forgot to charge his battery. He doesn't always check his messages, but I can try him again, get him to call you."

Max ruffled his thick, black hair, then met her eyes with a gaze so direct she had a foreboding of disaster. "I'll be honest with you. What your brother says won't make much difference."

"Because you've already made up your mind that he's guilty," she bit out, past trying to watch what she said. She needed to face up to the fact that he wasn't going to help.

"He is guilty. You said yourself that he sold somebody a forgery."

"I said he convinced himself it wasn't a forgery before he sold it."

He pushed back his chair from the table and stood up. He was at least six or seven inches taller than she was, but she didn't back down when he crossed the room. Neither did she take her eyes from his.

"You want to give your brother the benefit of the doubt. I get that. Johnny's lucky to have you in his corner. But I'm an FBI agent. I can't afford to believe every story I hear."

"So you think the worst of people?" She shook her head, not so much in anger as in sympathy. She hadn't blindly accepted her brother's story. He'd stayed clean for a full four years since his trouble with the law. He'd demonstrated he could be trusted. "It must be sad to live in a world where you can't give people the benefit of the doubt."

"I'm in law enforcement, Sara. Most of the people I meet have done bad things. They don't live in a vacuum. They're somebody's father. Or somebody's son. Or, yes, somebody's brother."

"You meet *strangers* who have done bad things. You don't know Johnny, but we're not only talking about my brother. We're talking about Larry, too. He's not a stranger."

"Sometimes the people we think we know the best are the ones who surprise us the most," he said in a soft voice, as though he believed the worst of Larry, too. Larry hadn't been the greatest boyfriend—in fact, he'd been quite a bad one. But if Sara could give him the benefit of the doubt, why couldn't Max?

"It's no use talking to you, is it? I don't know what I was thinking." She thumped her forehead. "Oh, yes, I do. Max is with the FBI. Max probably has experience in finding missing persons. Larry is missing. Surely Max will help find him."

He opened his mouth, but she beat him to the next sentence. "I didn't think you'd help because I asked you to. I thought you'd help because you and Larry go way back. I never dreamed you'd turn your back on a friend in need."

His expression remained so stoic that she felt like she was talking to an inanimate object, like the refrigerator humming gently in the corner of the room.

She shook her head and realized she had the beginnings of a headache. "I was so sure coming to you was the right move when I called Kevin and heard you were in town."

"Kevin said I'd help you find Larry?" He sounded surprised.

"I told you. Kevin wasn't home. I talked to his wife. I made the assumption myself. Oh, never mind." She threw up her hands, pivoted sharply on her summer sandals and headed for the door.

Max's attitude couldn't have been any more alien. Sara was hardwired to help the people who needed her. She'd thought the same of Max, and it hurt that she'd been mistaken.

"Where are you going?" he called after her.

"Back to town. I have a study session to go to and a man to find. It's obvious I made a mistake in coming here."

She heard footsteps behind her and would have disregarded them if his low, deep voice hadn't stopped her. "I didn't say I wouldn't help you."

The adrenaline charging through her veins went on hiatus. She stopped and turned to find him staring down at her, his brows knit, his strong features unreadable.

"Are you joking?" she asked.

"I seldom joke."

That, she could believe. "But if you were going to help, what was all that about back there?"

His Adam's apple bobbed as he swallowed and for the first time since she'd met him he didn't seem sure of himself. "That was about trying to figure out what I was getting myself in for."

"So you won't call the police?"

He swallowed again. "I won't call the police. But I also won't be a party to covering up a crime."

Because Sara didn't believe her brother had done anything worse than delude himself into thinking the autograph was real, she was willing to take that risk. "I understand."

"Tell me what you've done so far to try to find Larry," he said, sounding like the FBI agent he was.

"I stopped by his place and confirmed that his car was gone," she said. "I tried calling him but he dropped his cell phone last week and it stopped working. I don't think he got around to buying a new one."

She proceeded to fill him in on the people she'd talked to, which included Larry's co-workers, friends and family. Nobody knew where he'd gone, including Larry's parents and his sister, all of whom lived in Arizona.

"Are you working tonight?" he asked.

"My shift at Rusty's starts at six."

"I'll make some calls and catch up to you then. I want to talk to your co-workers myself," he said. "In the meantime, write down everything you can think of connected to Larry. Where he works. Where he lives. Where he shops. Names of friends. Neighbors. That kind of thing."

"Consider it done," she said, then impulsively reached for his hand and pressed it between both of hers. A shiver passed over her, telling her that touching him had been both the right and wrong thing to do. "Thank you."

Letting go of his hand, she walked quickly down the sidewalk, her skirt once again plastered to her legs to ward off the wind's blows. She doubted he'd go back on his word once he'd given it, but she didn't want to push her luck.

The sky was darker now, and the occasional fat raindrops splashed from above, giving her another reason to hurry.

"Sara." He called her name when she was halfway down the sidewalk. She turned to see him standing on the porch, staring after her. Thunder cracked, and Sara imagined the ground rumbled. "I'll need to talk to your brother, too."

The sky opened up, and relief washed over her along with the rain that he hadn't changed his mind. She ran for her car to escape the sheet of precipitation, one question pounding through her mind.

Why had he decided to help?

MAX SAT AT A CORNER TABLE at the Rusty Nail Pub on Saturday night, nursing a beer, watching two young guys with loud laughs and louder boasts trying to best each other at pool and wondering what the hell he'd gotten himself into.

He didn't need to wonder why he'd rushed head-long into a situation that smelled fishier than Baltimore's inner harbor.

He'd have agreed to damn near anything to stop

Sara from walking out the door and his life. Something about her drew him, like the city's megapopular National Aquarium attracted tourists.

Max had dated plenty of women but never for longer than a month or so before he lost interest. None of them had the same magnetic pull on him that Sara did. He wasn't entirely sure why that was. He liked looking at her, but there was more to it than that. Perhaps it was her caring nature and willingness to help anyone in need.

A part of him envied both Johnny and Larry. Max had never had a brother or sister to stand up for him. No girlfriend, present or former, who'd go to bat for him if he got into a jam.

A tidy little brunette with close-cropped curls, a heart-shaped face and a turned-up nose approached his table. Her girl-next-door looks were perfect for the pub, a friendly place where regulars sat on tall bar stools and watched ball games on overhead televisions.

"Sara said you wanted to talk to me. I'm Trixie Bennett."

"Yeah, that's right," Max said. "Thanks for making the time."

She pulled out the sturdy chair positioned at an angle from him and sat down. Like the table, the chair was fashioned out of heavy oak with warm, rich tones that went well with the lacquered wood floor.

"What I want to know is why you couldn't have wanted to talk to me last year. I'm freaking married now. Back then, I was only engaged. I'm not saying I would have been open to suggestion because I do love my husband, but the least you could have done was come in here and suggested."

Max felt a smile tug at the corner of his mouth. "I bet you say that to all the guys."

"Only if the guy's really hot or I think it'll get me a big tip." She balanced her elbows on the table and cupped her small, pointed chin. She looked about eighteen at first glance, but the faint lines around her nose and mouth put her nearer thirty. "Now what can I help you with?"

While Trixie had been making her introductions, a burly man no taller than five feet six moved from the front of the pub to the rear. Something about him seemed wrong, as though he were a square peg trying to fit into a round hole. He kept to himself, watching what went on around him but saying nothing.

"Before we get to that, take a look at the man by the pool table and tell me if you've seen him before."

Trixie swiveled her head. One of the boisterous young guys at the pool table badly missed an easy shot, earning grief from his friend. The short man didn't smile.

"The one who looks like a miniature Arnold Schwarzenegger? Yeah, he's been in here a couple of times this week. But I don't remember seeing him before then." Trixie turned back around, fastening vivid blue eyes on Max. "Why?"

"No reason."

Trixie narrowed her baby blues, turned to take another lingering look at the man and then snapped her fingers. "I get it. You're concerned because he's watching Sara."

Her powers of observation impressed Max. If he hadn't been aware of where Sara was in the bar at all times, he might not have noticed himself.

Not that Sara wasn't worth watching. She kept busy carrying plates of food from the kitchen and drinks from the bar to the grouping of tables where customers laughed, drank and ate.

She wore a red sleeveless shirt that outlined a very nice pair of breasts with low-waisted blue jeans that molded nicely to her rear end. She'd swept her long hair back into a haphazard knot, but sexy tendrils kept drifting into her face anyway.

Her gaze collided with his as she walked briskly to a booth while carrying two frothing mugs of beer. The smile she'd worn since arriving for her shift wavered, and the moment lengthened. Her step faltered, beer sloshed from a mug onto one of her hands and she broke eye contact.

Max focused once again on Trixie. "You're very perceptive."

"It's no big deal. Lots of men watch Sara." Trixie studied him. "You've been doing it yourself."

"She's worth watching," Max said simply, then changed the subject before she could share any more observations. "Did Sara tell you why I wanted to talk to you?"

"After I browbeat it out of her, she did. Although I'm pretty sure she hasn't told anyone else. Sara doesn't usually talk about her problems and she's real protective of her brother. But, yeah, I know about the fake autograph and I know Larry and the money are missing."

Max relaxed his guard a little. If Sara had told Trixie about Johnny's troubles, she obviously trusted her. "Any idea where Larry might be?"

"I answered the phone when he called. He said

he was going to visit a sick aunt, but I gather he doesn't have one. So my guess is he took a vacation. But I don't know where to."

"Has Larry lied to get out of work before?"

"I'm sure he has."

Trixie's theory that Larry had taken an impromptu vacation was also taking root in Max's mind, but he couldn't ignore the possibility that something else had sent Larry packing.

"Do you find it odd that Larry didn't let anyone know where he was going and that no one can reach him?"

Trixie shrugged. "Larry's not the most conscientious of men. I don't think anything bad has happened to him, if that's what you're getting at. I think he'll turn up when he wants to."

That seemed to be the overwhelming consensus among Larry's friends and relatives. That afternoon Max had worked the phones, contacting mutual friends who kept in touch with Larry as well as his parents and sister in Arizona.

Not a single person had heard from Larry but neither had anybody seemed concerned. Larry sometimes took off for days at a time, he'd heard over and over again. It didn't mean anything.

"How much leeway will the owner give him before he's in danger of losing his job?" Max asked.

"Didn't Sara tell you?" Trixie's expressive blue eyes conveyed her surprise. "Rusty opened another location in Philadelphia a few weeks ago so he's spending the month there. Sara's in charge while he's away."

Max frowned, mentally crossing Rusty off the list of the people he needed to question while thinking up a couple new questions for Sara. "Would Larry be afraid that Sara would report him to the boss?"

Trixie rolled her eyes. "Hardly. Sara's been fixing Larry's problems since they met. Why would she stop now?"

"I get the impression you don't like Larry."

She made a face. "I don't. Part of the reason is because I do like Sara, and trouble follows Larry around. I mean, look at the mess he's in right now. Even if it turns out he's a victim of circumstances, and I'd be surprised if he was, it's still trouble. Too bad Sara didn't stay away from him from the start."

Max had entertained that same thought, but couldn't fault Sara. He'd been watching women fall for Larry for years. "Larry can turn on the charm when he wants to."

"You're right about that. And he's handsome, on top of it. But I don't think that's why Sara dated him. I think it was because she wanted to solve his problems."

A movement at the back of the bar diverted Max's attention. The muscle man set down his empty beer mug on a nearby table, took one more lingering look at Sara, then waddled toward the exit with that peculiar gait common to men who spend too much time in the gym.

The door to the bar opened onto the street, and another man tried to enter the pub. Mini Arnold didn't give an inch, shouldering past the other man, who had to move out of the way.

Don't mess with me, his body language screamed.

When the man was out of sight, Max returned his attention to Trixie. "What problems?"

"His money problems, for one. Larry spends more than he makes. When he and Sara were together, she was always trying to get him to budget his money and cut up his credit cards."

"Did she lend him money?"

Trixie drummed the table with her fingertips. "I don't think so. She's as broke as any of us, what with her going to Johns Hopkins. But she was certainly willing to help him out. Why else would she have let him live with her even after they broke up?"

Max tried to make his voice casual although the new piece of information had jarred him. "I didn't know she had."

Trixie nodded. "Took him way too long to find an apartment, too. Let's see. Sara broke up with Larry in April and he didn't move out until July. Like I said, he's needy. And from the sound of it, it seems like he still needs her."

Max found it ironic that he had only to look at Sara to wish that Larry Brunell was out of the picture and now here he was trying to bring the other man back into it. He didn't want to ask the next question but found he couldn't hold it back. "Are you saying that Sara wants to get back together with Larry?"

"Oh, no." Trixie's eyes rounded, as though she were as horrified by the thought as Max was. "But I'll tell you something else. Don't expect Sara to stop worrying about him or caring about him, because that's not going to happen. That's just Sara. Once somebody's in her life, they're in."

"Even a bad boyfriend?"

"That's the thing about Sara." Trixie took a beer

nut from the small wooden bowl on the table and popped it into her mouth. "She notices the bad but still keeps searching for the good."

3

MAX AND LARRY WEREN'T friends any longer.

Sara had inadvertently discovered that fact an hour ago when she'd checked her cell phone and discovered that Kevin Carmichael had returned last night's call.

She'd taken a moment to go outside the bar and call Kevin back, only to learn the newlywed hadn't heard from Larry and wasn't particularly concerned by his disappearing act. Before Kevin had hung up, he'd suggested a couple other people Sara could call.

Max Dolinger's in town but don't bother trying him, Kevin had said. *It would be a waste of time.*

Yet Max had been on Larry's trail for a good eight hours. Max stood next to her even now, waiting to cross the street to the small park across from the pub so they could talk in private. About Larry, she presumed.

The question she'd yet to ask him crowded her mind, more of a puzzler than ever now that she knew he and Larry were no longer buddies.

Why had Max agreed to help?

Sara wiped her damp palms on the legs of her jeans, annoyed at herself for being nervous about what the answer might be.

A daring, fanciful part of her she'd only recently

discovered wanted his motive to be personal, but the realist in her understood that would create a problem.

Max Dolinger fascinated her because he was forceful, self-sufficient and thus utterly unlike the men who usually gravitated toward her. But that magnetism also made him a very big distraction.

She frowned, recognizing the irony of being distracted by the very man who represented her best chance at finding Larry.

A dark-colored SUV sped up the street, and Max laid a hand on her arm, as though making sure she didn't pick the wrong moment to step off the curb.

She liked that he kept his hand on her arm as they walked to one of the cast-iron benches in the little slice of parkland that marked the center of O'Donnell Square.

Flanked by a stone church and an old fire station, the grassy strip divided O'Donnell Street in half. Traffic on the northern portion of the road flowed west while cars traveling on the southern part headed east.

The Rusty Nail Pub was among an eclectic mix of specialty stores that included a TV-and-radio repair shop, a discount liquor store and a pretzel shop. With its brick facade and flower baskets that hung from the windows, Rusty's had instantly charmed Sara, but the park was the best part of the park.

They passed the statue of Irish sea captain John O'Donnell, who stood imperiously over the square as though he still owned the land on which it stood. The bench nearest the statue was slightly damp from the day's rain, but she sat down anyway.

Only then did Max's hand slip from her arm.

"I asked Trixie to cover for me, but I shouldn't

take more than a ten-minute break," she said. "It's pretty busy tonight."

"This won't take long."

He sat down beside her, but not so closely that her stomach should have jumped the way it did. The night made his hair look as black as coal and his skin seemed pale in comparison. He didn't wear cologne but smelled wonderfully male. She couldn't remember the last time she'd been so aware of a man.

"Thanks for the list." He patted the pocket of his khaki pants. So far she'd seen him in formal wear, yard clothes and khakis. She wondered if he ever kicked back in a T-shirt and pair of blue jeans. "I'll have plenty of people to talk to tomorrow. Nobody I contacted today knew much."

"Did you check with the airlines yet to see if Larry bought a ticket somewhere?"

"I'm not going to call the airlines," Max said.

"But why not? That's what happens on TV when the FBI's trying to find a missing person."

"It can't happen in real life unless the person is officially missing, which Larry isn't. Even then, you need a court order to prove the information is relevant to a criminal investigation."

"Does that mean you can't check his credit-card purchases, either?"

"Again, not unless he's officially missing. Banks—and airlines—have policies in place to protect the privacy of their customers."

"Oh." Sara hadn't considered that there would be red tape Max wouldn't be able to cut through. "Then how will you find him?"

"The old-fashioned way." Max stretched his legs

out in front of him, crossing them at the ankles, and she noticed how long they were. "By talking to people who know him and pursuing whatever leads I come up with. Your brother's still at the top of my list of people to talk to."

At the mention of her brother, she felt a twinge of guilt. She still hadn't told him about Johnny's past, but she couldn't risk prejudicing him before he'd met her brother. After Max saw for himself that Johnny was a good person, then she'd tell him.

"I keep getting no answer when I try his cell, but he left a message on my voice mail that he was spending the night with a friend." She felt compelled to add, "This isn't normal for him. He's usually quite reachable."

He quirked a dark eyebrow, but she wasn't sure whether that meant he'd accepted her explanation or that he hadn't. Just in case he hadn't, she changed the subject.

"Did you come up with any leads today?" she asked.

He turned toward her. This afternoon's storm had blown over, but there wasn't much of a moon and his face was partially in shadows.

"A couple," he said. "I heard you were managing the bar this month with the owner gone."

"That's true, but how is that a lead?"

"It's not a lead, per se. But it could have been a factor in Larry's decision to go AWOL. With you in charge instead of the pub owner, he'd be less likely to get in trouble if his excuse was discovered to be bogus."

Sara frowned, not sure she followed his logic. "How is that relevant?"

"It's starting to seem likely that Larry wanted to take some time off, saw an opportunity and grabbed it."

She nodded, wishing Larry had said something in the past few months about places he'd like to visit.

"What other lead do you have?" she asked.

"A number of people I talked to said Larry was having money problems."

She considered that. "I don't think any more than usual. But Larry likes to spend. Clothes. Dinners. Movies. He never has enough money." She stopped abruptly as a reason for Max's question occurred to her. "Do you think Larry owed someone?"

"It's a theory. It would explain why he came up with the scheme to sell the baseball." Although his voice was mild, his choice of words wasn't.

"Don't you think *scheme* is the wrong word?"

"Not really." He shrugged. "Even if Larry believed the autograph was genuine, the baseball wasn't his. By my count, Larry's cut was seventy-five hundred. He did locate the buyer, but that's quite a haul for a finder's fee."

"And you think he did all this because he had debts to repay?"

"Like I said, it's a theory. It could be wrong. He could be spending the money on a vacation."

That scenario wasn't much more palatable. Because if Larry was going through the money, where did that leave Johnny? Sara didn't have anywhere near seventy-five hundred dollars in the bank and she couldn't qualify for a loan. Asking her parents for money was out because they'd spent their windfall and had little left.

"I don't know for sure that Larry's already spent

the money, Sara," he said as though he'd read her
mind. "And I don't know where he went or why he
left in such a rush. But you can be sure of one thing.
I'll keep looking for him until I do."

"But why?" The question escaped her lips before
Sara fully realized she meant to ask it. It hung there
in the air between them, but she didn't want to take
it back.

She shifted positions on the park bench, angling
her body toward him, and breathed in the lingering
scent of the day's rain—and Max.

Even though the scattering of pubs up and down
O'Donnell Street were doing a fair business, nobody
besides she and Max were in the square. Somewhere
down the block, a woman laughed. A car that needed
muffler work clanked by. He met her gaze but said
nothing.

"Kevin returned my call a little while ago," she
continued. "He mentioned that you and Larry aren't
friends anymore."

A long pause. "That's true."

"Then why are you helping him?" she persisted.

The wind blew hair into her face, and he brushed
back strands that had come loose from her topknot.
Only the pads of his fingers touched her cheek, but
her whole body felt the contact.

"I'm not helping Larry," he said softly. "I'm helping you."

She couldn't see all his features clearly, but she
could see his mouth. The lower lip was slightly fuller
than the upper, which was bowed in the middle,
enough to make it sensuous, not enough to make
him appear any less masculine.

She wanted to kiss him, she realized.

What's more, this crazy attraction wasn't new. It had flared to life at the wedding, when she'd noticed Max's friends held him in high regard and watched to discover why that was. She'd seen a man both cool enough to deal with a drunk and kind enough to dance with the stooped, white-haired grandmother of the bride.

But she and Larry had been together then so she hadn't dared admit, even to herself, how strongly attracted she was to Max.

She admitted it now.

No part of his body touched hers, but his eyes seemed to caress her. Heat spread low in her belly, and she held her breath as she waited for him to close the narrow gap between their mouths and press his beautiful lips to hers.

A car horn blared. Sara blinked, jolted out of the fantasy. Max hadn't moved except for a muscle that jumped in his jaw. He certainly hadn't tried to kiss her.

"You should get back to work before Trixie comes looking for you," he said.

She stood up on legs that suddenly felt shaky, wondering if she had misread the situation. But no, he'd definitely stated she was the reason he'd agreed to look for Larry.

This time when they walked through the park and across the street, he didn't take her arm. The silence between them was so absolute that she imagined she could hear the hum of insects in the trees overhead. She was about to step across the threshold into the pub when he said her name.

Looking back at him over her shoulder, she tried not to notice the sensuous curve to his mouth. Oh,

Lord, the man had a beautiful mouth. His night-dark eyes met hers.

"I'd like for you to understand something, Sara," he said in a voice as soft as the velvety darkness. "I'm not helping you because I think I can get something from you. I'm helping you because you need help."

A shiver traveled the length of her body. She waitressed at a pub where men constantly complimented her—on her figure, on her personality, on her eyes, on her smile.

But in twenty-four years, that was hands down the most romantic thing anybody had ever said to her.

MAX RUBBED AT HIS BLEARY EYES, checking the face of his watch even though he already knew the time. Saturday night had finally ended, and it was now technically Sunday morning. Nearly 2:00 a.m. on Sunday morning, to be exact.

He should be asleep in his childhood bedroom but instead sat in his car on a darkened patch of street outside Rusty's keeping what so far had been an unnecessary vigil.

He'd been ready to call it a night hours ago, shortly after he and Sara had talked in O'Donnell Square. But when he'd gotten in his car, he couldn't bring himself to turn the key in the ignition.

His uneasy feeling about the man who'd been in the pub earlier that evening wouldn't let him.

So he'd kept watch, looking for signs of somebody lurking in the shadows. But so far the city block had been quiet except for the few dozen or so stragglers who'd trickled out of Rusty's.

The only one doing any lurking tonight, it seemed, was Max.

He finished the bag of M&M's he'd kept stashed in his glove compartment, crumpled the wrapper and stuck it in his pocket.

Sara would certainly be surprised that he was still here. He'd told her neither about the man in the pub who'd been watching her or his plan to make sure she got home safely.

He'd meant what he'd said. His help didn't come with strings attached, and he was loathe to make her feel indebted to him.

He let his head fall back against the headrest, thinking about how hard it had been to stop from kissing her earlier tonight, frustrated about the corner he'd backed himself into.

If he kissed her now, she might think he hadn't been telling the truth.

Eventually Sara walked out of the bar with Trixie, her fair-colored head bent toward Trixie's darker one, her expression serious. Max's gaze combed the dark places the streetlights didn't illuminate but still he saw no one.

The two women paused in front of the large picture window that had The Rusty Nail Pub stenciled across it, with Trixie doing most of the talking. The street lamp caught Sara's face, infusing it with light and warmth.

Sara rubbed Trixie's arm soothingly, her attention focused entirely on the shorter woman. They talked for a few more minutes before Sara enveloped Trixie in a warm hug, then walked to an older-model Saab parked well up the street.

Trixie headed for a Civic two parking spaces in front of Max's rental car. Max slumped against the back of the driver's seat, but Trixie seemed more interested in getting home than checking out her surroundings.

She sped off, with Sara soon following at a slower pace. After waiting a few measured seconds, Max followed Sara's Saab through the darkened streets for about a mile until she stopped in front of a row house with a green door and boxes spilling over with daisies.

Like the pub, the row house was in Canton, an older neighborhood east of the Inner Harbor that had become a favorite of young, urban professionals and where reasonably priced rentals were rare.

Sara's slice of the neighborhood boasted Baltimore's famed marble stoops, but the dwellings here were more modest than those near O'Donnell Square.

Max pulled to the curb across from her place, watching her get out of the Saab and shut the door. Her car was too old to have a remote, so she manually locked the car door before heading up the sidewalk.

The occasional car passed by but otherwise the street was quiet, with nothing to arouse suspicion. Max started to think his sixth sense had steered him wrong.

Three marble steps and an iron railing led to her gaily painted front door. Sara approached with keys in hand, then hesitated as though something had surprised her.

Max squinted to get a better look at the door and realized it was slightly ajar. A warning signal blared in his brain, as loud and urgent as a siren. Every muscle in his body went taut.

"Don't go in there, Sara," he said aloud, but she took a step inside the apartment.

Cold fear slithered through him like a venomous snake. He pulled his .40-caliber Glock semiautomatic from his ankle holster, yanked open the door and hit the pavement running.

SARA SIGHED AUDIBLY at the sight of the partially open front door. Life with a teenager was never boring.

After the message Johnny had left on her cell, she hadn't expected him to be home. She certainly hadn't anticipated that he'd forget to pull the door all the way shut.

There had to be an explanation, of course. Johnny was a good kid, but he was a teenager. He made mistakes. He could have been tired. Or careless. Or—and she hoped this wasn't the case—drunk. She hadn't seen him drink since he'd moved in with her two months ago, but Johnny had had a problem with peer pressure in the past. If the people he'd been with tonight had been drinking, he could have downed a few.

Pushing the door the rest of the way open, she ventured a few steps inside. Her hand curled around the edge of the door, preparing to swing it closed behind her, but for some reason she hesitated.

"Johnny?" she called. No answer. "Are you home, Johnny?"

The layout was typical of a Baltimore row house, long and narrow with the living room taking up the front portion of the first floor and the kitchen the back.

The owner was an elderly woman Sara had be-friended before starting nursing school. Sara had been working a temp job as a receptionist in the doctor's office where the woman was a patient. When the woman's failing health made it necessary for her to move in with family, she'd rented to Sara.

Hardly a day went by that Sara didn't appreciate her good luck in stumbling across the charming little place, but tonight the row house seemed sinister.

The living-room lamp didn't shed enough light to reach the darkened corners of the front room, and all Sara could make out of the kitchen were the glowing numbers on the microwave clock. She could barely see the staircase that led north to the two bedrooms on the upper floor and south to the basement.

Logic told her everything was as it should be. Johnny had probably arrived home hours ago and turned in for the night, for whatever reason not realizing the door was ajar.

Partly mollified by the explanation, she released the air that had been trapped in her lungs. And heard heavy, rapid footsteps thunder down the oak stairs.

She froze. The footsteps didn't sound as though they belonged to Johnny, who was slight of build and not overly tall.

Her heart beating hard, she backed up toward the front door just as a man emerged from the staircase. The soft glow from the lamp didn't fully illuminate his features but he was too tall and muscular to be Johnny.

He held a small, dark object in his hand. A gun?

She opened her mouth to scream but the breath

caught in her lungs. Adrenaline pumped through her in a sickening rush, unfreezing her muscles. Turning, she fled blindly for the open door.

4

MAX BURST THROUGH the door, only to collide with an onrushing Sara.

He managed to keep his balance while she screamed and pushed at his chest. Careful to keep his gun averted, he gripped her shoulders. She reared back her right foot and kicked him hard in the shins.

"Ow! Jeez, Sara. Stop. It's Max."

Her eyes flew to his. He felt some of the tension leave her body as she recognized him but still read panic on her face, which had gone as white as the marble stoop of her porch.

"A man. He was upstairs. Still here," she sputtered.

He looked over her shoulder into the row house. The living room was clearly visible but he could only see a portion of what appeared to be a large kitchen at the back of the house.

He pulled the door shut and quickly reversed their positions so Sara was behind him. Holding his weapon in front of him, he took in the layout of the apartment. "Is he armed?"

"I'm not sure, but I think so."

The squeak of protesting hinges gave away the man's location. The back door. Max resisted his impulse to dash for the kitchen and rush after the man.

Chances are the intruder was working alone but Max couldn't risk it.

"Don't move," he told Sara, careful to keep his sights on both the back of the row house and the staircase. The bedrooms would be upstairs. So, too, could be another intruder.

He gave the kitchen a thorough once-over, caught Sara's eye and pantomimed the motion of dialing a phone. When he was fairly certain she understood his message to call 9-1-1, he nodded toward the staircase.

Squinting to get his eyes accustomed to the darkness, he crept silently up the stairs, listening for any sounds that would give away the location of a second perpetrator. Hearing nothing, he flicked on the hall light when he reached the second floor. Two bedrooms did indeed take up the entire floor. In seconds he'd determined that nobody was inside either of them.

Not daring to leave Sara alone an instant longer than necessary, Max hurried down the stairs. She was on the phone, explaining what had happened to the dispatcher. Again he caught her attention and indicated the stairs leading south.

Flipping a light switch, he descended, gun at the ready. He went through the motions, searching the finished sitting room, the washer/dryer area and small bathroom. But he already knew that only a single man had been inside Sara's apartment.

That man was long gone.

When he reappeared on the main floor, he could hear the distant sound of police sirens. Sara stood in the middle of the living room, hugging her midsection.

"All clear," he said, returning his Glock to his ankle holster so the cops wouldn't mistake him for the perp. "Did you tell the dispatcher an FBI agent was already on the scene?"

She nodded but didn't speak.

His heart beat hard in delayed reaction, not because he'd been afraid for himself, but because he'd been afraid for Sara. He crossed the room in two strides.

"Damn it, Sara, don't you know not to go into your house if you suspect a break-in?"

"But I didn't suspect anything," Sara protested. "I thought Johnny had come home and, I don't know, not realized he hadn't pulled the door entirely closed."

"Johnny's not here," Max pointed out. "Nobody is."

"I know that now." Her voice held strength, but her lower lip trembled and he realized too late that she was making an effort to hold herself together.

"You're shaking," he said.

"I am not." Even as she vehemently denied his accusation, her voice quavered. "Well, maybe I am a little. But that's understandable. I was scared out of my mind."

Her big, brown eyes were his undoing. They were dry, but filled with a vulnerability he'd never seen before.

He drew her to him with one long arm, half expecting her to protest that she was fine now that the threat was past. But she accepted his embrace, resting her cheek against his chest while he ran a soothing hand over her back.

He liked the feel of her against him, liked knowing he'd been able to keep her safe and that she trusted him enough to let him offer comfort.

The interlude lasted no more than thirty seconds

before she drew back, no longer seeming the least bit shaky. Her eyes were once again clear, the vulnerability gone, the transformation nothing short of amazing.

"Sorry about that," she said as though she had anything to apologize for. "I don't usually come home to find a strange man in my apartment."

Because he still wanted to hold her, he shoved his hands into his pockets. "I'm the one who's sorry. I shouldn't have snapped at you. But when I saw you go through that front door, my heart almost stopped."

Small frown lines appeared between her eyebrows. "I thought you went home hours ago. How did you happen to be here tonight?"

He shrugged. "I didn't like the way a guy at the bar was looking at you, so I followed you to make sure you got home safely."

"What did this guy look like?"

"Short, muscular, seems like he spends a lot of time in the gym."

"I didn't notice him, but that's not the guy who broke in." She kneaded her forehead, as though the motion would help her remember the description of the man. "This guy was powerfully built, but tall. I'd say six feet two, maybe even taller."

The sirens had grown increasingly louder as they spoke, the responding patrol car seeming to have reached the same block as the row house. Max turned but Sara reached out to put a hand on his arm, stopping him from heading for the front door.

"Max, I need to ask you a favor." She dropped her hand and ran it through her hair, which had come loose from her topknot. Smudges of fatigue darkened the area under her eyes. "Would you not mention the trouble Johnny's in?"

Her eyes were round and beseeching, her mouth slightly parted as she waited for his answer.

He doubted the cops would delve too deeply into what had happened tonight. He'd been upstairs and it didn't look as though anything had been stolen.

Still, he hesitated. What if he'd missed something in his cursory search?

"Have you ever had a break-in before tonight?" he asked.

She shook her head, her answer giving him more reason to confide in the police. The break-in had come too close on the heels of the sale of the bogus baseball to make him comfortable in labeling it a coincidence.

The noise abruptly stopped, and red and blue lights flashed through the front window in a revolving pattern. Within seconds, the police would come pounding on the door.

"You won't say anything about Johnny, will you?" Sara asked, her tone imploring.

Something inside his chest went soft, or maybe it was something inside his head. Damn.

"Okay," he said. "I won't mention Johnny."

Max didn't know either of the uniformed cops who responded to the 9-1-1 call but they were amenable enough to having him tag along while they went through the apartment.

Within minutes, they'd reached a conclusion Max couldn't argue with.

"Looks like you interrupted a burglary," the older

cop told Sara. He was middle-aged and florid-faced, with gray hair the texture of a brillo pad and a belly that had gone soft.

"As far as we could tell, he didn't take anything." His partner was maybe twenty-three, with a face so fresh he looked like he passed up the coffee and doughnuts and went straight for the milk.

Sara had already confirmed that nothing seemed to be missing. Her most valuable possessions—diamond earrings and a pearl necklace she'd inherited from her grandmother—were still nestled safely inside the wooden jewelry box on her bedroom dresser.

"We put out the guy's description over the radio but there's nothing more we can do," the young cop added.

Like his partner, he seemed eager to be on his way. Max couldn't blame either of them. Saturday night in the city was always busy, with most calls turning out to be much more serious than this one.

But Max wasn't comfortable writing off the incident as a botched burglary. None of the lights had been left on upstairs, so he agreed with the cops' supposition that the object Sara had seen in the man's hand had been a flashlight rather than a gun.

But why hadn't the man turned on the lights and searched for valuables? It could be because Sara had surprised him before he got started, but that brought up another question.

If he hadn't intended to use force to get what he wanted, why hadn't he broken in during the day when the residence was more likely to be unoccupied?

"Have there been many break-ins in this neighbor-hood lately?" Max asked.

The older cop scratched his chin. "No more than usual. But the short dead bolt on the front door made this place an easy target. A hard blow popped it right open." He nodded to Sara. "You should get that lock replaced, ma'am."

"I will," she said. "Thank you."

The two policemen acknowledged her gratitude with a nod and left. Sara waited until they were gone, the door shut behind them, before she spoke. "Thanks for not saying anything about Johnny."

The policemen had been in such a hurry, he doubted it would have made any difference if he had. "You heard them. They think this was a stray incident."

"Do you believe that?"

Max stroked his chin, considering her question. "I can't see how it would be connected to the baseball. Johnny has a deadline of Friday to return the money, right?"

She nodded.

"Then the man who bought the ball wouldn't have a reason to break in, not even if he suspected Johnny was lying about not having the rest of the money. He only has to wait a few more days until he gets it all."

"That's what I thought, too," she said, keeping the proverbial stiff upper lip.

But Max was good at reading people. She wasn't as unrattled as she pretended. Her color still hadn't returned to normal, her lower lip had a barely per-ceptible tremble and she kept wringing her hands.

"I'll move something in front of the door after you

leave," she said. "I shouldn't have any more problems tonight, not after the police have been here."

She didn't know him very well if she thought he'd go off into the night after what had happened.

"You can't stay here by yourself," Max said.

"But I can't leave, either." Her voice sounded as tired as the rest of her looked. "Not with the lock broken. Everything I own is inside this apartment. I know it's not much but—"

"I didn't mean you should leave," Max interrupted. "I meant I should stay."

THE BRAVE FRONT Sara had erected since finding the intruder crumbled and her knees went weak with relief. She hadn't realized how much she'd dreaded spending the night alone until Max made his declaration.

The soft light washed over him, causing his hair and eyes to appear even darker than they did in the sunshine. Strength and competence rolled off him in waves.

"It's not safe in here with the lock broken," Max continued. "I'll put some furniture in front of the door and sleep on the sofa. In the morning, I'll call a locksmith and make sure he installs the right kind of locks."

She nearly told him that she could take care of herself. She'd done it for years. She could do it again. She could barricade the door to keep trouble out. Come morning, she could meet with the locksmith.

But she kept silent because, for once, it felt good not to have to shoulder all of her burdens alone.

"It's been a long day and you look tired," he said, his dark eyes soft. "You should get some rest."

She was tired. She'd been on her feet all night, and she hadn't sat down since discovering the intruder in her house. Her legs probably wouldn't hold her for much longer.

"That table against the wall is fairly heavy," she said, nodding in the direction of a sturdy mahogany piece the owner had left behind. "I can help you move it in front of the door."

"I'll do it after you go to sleep," he said. "All I need is a pillow and a blanket. Just tell me where to find them."

"On the upper shelf in the hall closet," she answered, "but it really won't be a problem for me to get them for you."

"Let me do it," he said, touching her cheek. "Please."

Something inside her softened, then spread. Most of the other people in her life wanted something from her, but Max hadn't made any demands.

"I appreciated what you said tonight," she said, "about how you weren't angling to get anything from me."

"I meant it."

She wet her lips. The lateness of the hour, combined with the dark, moonless night outside the door, added an intimate quality to the room. The silence stretched. The air seemed to grow thicker, the tick of the mantle clock louder, the hum of the refrigerator more prevalent.

Even though she was exhausted, she didn't want the night to end. She wanted him to kiss her. The moment lengthened, and she knew he wasn't going to.

"Well, goodnight, Max," she said, hoping she was wrong.

"Goodnight, Sara," he said softly.

Sara gave him one last long look before walking to the stairs, all the while fighting the urge to turn around and go back to him.

5

TURN AROUND, Max silently urged as Sara reached the first step. He'd charged to her rescue earlier tonight, but now he was honor bound to stand his ground.

He needed her to make the first move. If he made it, his claim that he wasn't aiming to get something from her would mean nothing.

Turn around, he urged again as she paused on the second step.

She turned.

He didn't dare move. She seemed to float toward him, and he had to fight to keep from reaching for her. She stopped in front of him, her eyes intent on his, then put a hand to his nape and pulled his head down to hers.

Her lips were as sweet as they looked, but not nearly as innocent. She kissed him hungrily, nipping at his bottom lip, laving her tongue over his top lip. Her arms encircled his neck, her soft breasts pressed against his chest and she molded her lower body to him.

He opened his mouth and kissed her back, no longer worried about letting her see how much he wanted her. This was a woman who could match him kiss for kiss, heartbeat for heartbeat, stroke for stroke.

She kissed him for a few more mindless moments before tearing her mouth from his and gazing at him with passion-glazed eyes.

"Come upstairs with me, Max," she invited in a throaty voice before breaking away from him and taking his hand.

His heart pounding with anticipation, he let her lead him up the stairs.

Thud. Thud. Thud.

The noise jarred him. He didn't understand. Was that the sound of his footsteps on the stairs? The beating of his heart?

Thud. Thud. Thud.

He tried opening his eyes to see what was going on, but his eyelids felt heavy. Sara still tugged his hand. He held on, not wanting to let go. But the thudding wouldn't stop.

His eyes snapped open, and Sara disappeared. He was no longer on the staircase but lying flat on his back, his legs tangled in a blanket.

Rays of weak sunlight banished the night, illuminating an unfamiliar room decorated with heavy mahogany furniture and upholstery with chintz patterns.

Thud. Thud. Thud.

Max sat bolt upright, realizing he'd been dreaming. Sara hadn't changed her mind and come to him last night. It had all been a fantasy.

The events of the night before came rushing back. He was sleeping on the sofa at Sara's, because the lock on her front door was broken.

And somebody was at the front door.

Hell, how had he gotten so lost in a dream that

he'd let down his guard? Cursing himself, he reached for the gun he'd laid on the coffee table last night before he fell asleep.

"Sara," a male voice called through a slim crack between the heavy front door and the table preventing it from opening. "Are you in there, Sara? I can't get in."

Guessing that the person at the door was Sara's elusive brother, Max relaxed and holstered the gun at his ankle. Then he swiped a hand over his brow and tried to shake off the effects of the dream.

He was some hero, he thought in disgust. True, he wasn't angling to get anything from Sara. But he sure wouldn't refuse anything she offered.

He untangled his legs from the blanket and got to his feet, smoothing the wrinkles in the clothes he'd slept in. Then he went to put a stop to the thudding.

"Just a minute," he called through the crack in the door.

He lifted the heavy table, being careful not to scratch the finish on the wood floor as he moved it to the side. Then he pulled open the door.

Yeah, it was Sara's kid brother all right. The coloring was the same—light-colored hair, brown eyes, fair skin. But this kid didn't have the weary look that sometimes came into his sister's eyes. His hair was cut short and neat, his eyes were bright, his skin glowing with health.

He looked like the quintessential all-American boy, one who'd be perfect in a commercial advertising clothes for a store like Old Navy.

"You're Johnny Reynolds, right?"

"That's right." The kid's bright eyes, a much lighter shade of brown than Sara's, narrowed. He was average height and on the slim side but looked ready to do battle. "But who are you? And what have you done with my sister?"

Max stifled an urge to smile at his dramatic choice of words. "I'm Max Dolinger, and your sister's upstairs. Asleep, I think."

"Dolinger." His expression cleared. "You're the FBI agent she went to see yesterday. The one she was going to try to convince to help us."

"You should thank her for that."

"I want to thank you first, too, Agent Dolinger." Johnny stuck out his hand.

"Call me Max," Max said, noting and approving of the firmness of his grip.

When they were done shaking, Johnny looked beyond him to the rumpled sheets on the sofa, then sideways to the table that had barricaded the door. "I don't understand what's going on. What are you doing here? And what happened to the door?"

"There was some trouble last night. Sara surprised an intruder when she got home from work. He's the one who broke the door."

"Is Sara okay?" the kid asked anxiously, taking a few steps toward the staircase.

"She's fine. He ran out the back door when I came through the front."

Johnny let out a relieved breath. "Oh, man. But that's wild. Plenty of the neighbors have more than us. Why would anyone break into our place?"

Max folded his arms across his chest while he regarded Johnny. "I'm not entirely convinced this was a burglary attempt. Not with everything else that's been going on."

Johnny had been looking him straight in the eyes but now glanced away. He cleared his throat. "You know about the baseball, then?"

"I know the man you sold it to wants his money back. What I want to know is if he's unhappy enough to break in here looking for it."

Johnny's eyes swung back to his. "Ralph? No way."

"How can you be so sure?"

"The man's seventy years old. I don't see him popping locks and breaking into houses."

Another red flag went up, adding weight to Max's suspicion that Johnny and Larry had deliberately scammed the buyer. Con artists targeted senior citizens more than people in any other age group, partly because they had more disposable income.

"I'll tell you anything you want to know," Johnny said, "but can I make coffee first?"

Sara came into the kitchen before the coffee was ready, her complexion rosy from sleep, her mouth soft with it. Her hair fell down around her shoulders in disarray, and her nubby yellow robe covered everything but her bare feet with their pink-painted toenails.

Max thought she looked sexier than hell.

"Good morning." She included both of them in her smile. "I heard voices so I came downstairs to investigate."

A mug in hand, Johnny left the cabinet door open and went to his sister's side. "Sara, I heard what happened. Are you really okay?"

"I'm fine, Johnny." A wash of sunlight caught her face and highlighted the faint sprinkling of freckles across her nose. She touched her brother's shoulder.

"It was you I was worried about when I couldn't get you on the phone."

"I didn't know my battery was dead until I tried to call you. You did get my message that I wasn't coming home last night, right?"

She nodded, going over to the counter and turning off the coffeepot. She took the mug from Johnny, removed two more from the cabinet and filled all three with the steaming brew.

After adding cream and sugar to two of them, she said to Max, "No cream, extra sugar. Right?"

Most people assumed he took it black. "How did you know that?" Max asked.

"Lucky guess," she said with a smile, then looked from him to her brother. "I gather the two of you introduced yourselves."

"Yeah. Agent Dolinger…" Johnny stopped himself, started again, "…Max wanted to ask me some questions."

She distributed the mugs of coffee, then joined them at the table, making it clear she intended to sit in on the interview. Damn. People were usually more forthcoming without family members in the room.

"I want to hear what happened," Max said, nodding in the boy's direction. "From the beginning."

"The very beginning?" Johnny seemed to cast his mind back. "I guess that would be when Larry showed me Barbarellen."

"Barbarellen's a silly nickname Larry has for his prized possession," Sara explained. "It's a bronze sculpture of a female stick figure holding up a barbell. He bought it a couple years ago from a sculptor who's since done very well for himself."

"It's way cool," Johnny said. "But I said my auto-graphed Babe Ruth baseball was cooler. I never thought he'd get so excited about it. I've showed that autograph to a lot of guys, but I think Larry's the first one who believed Babe Ruth really signed it."

"So you never thought the autograph was authentic?"

"Heck, no."

Max wondered if the kid hadn't sworn because Sara was in the room or if he really was as whole-some as he seemed.

"Well, maybe when I was real young, before my dad told me it was a fake," Johnny amended. "I still kept it, though, because it was fun trying to fool my friends."

Before Max could ask what had changed his mind about the autograph's validity, Sara interjected, "Larry convinced Johnny the autograph might be real. He said the authenticator our father took the ball to could have been the fake instead of the signature. He could have lied to get the ball for a rock-bottom price."

Max bit back a sigh. This was why he didn't like having family members in the room during ques-tioning. He gentled his voice to take the sting out of his words. "Sara, could you let Johnny tell it?"

"Sorry," she said.

Johnny went on to relate basically the same story that Sara had, complete with the deal he'd cut with Larry to split the profits.

When he was through, Max leaned back in the kitchen chair, kneading his brow. "Back up to the part where Larry insisted on being paid with a cash-ier's check. Why did he do that?"

"He said checks bounced, cashier's checks didn't."

"How about the price? Why did you set it so high?"

"Isn't the value of an item the price the buyer's willing to pay?" Sara asked before her brother could respond.

Christ, she was protective.

"Can I say something, Mr. Dolinger, I mean Max?" The kid had a nice way about him, a direct way of looking you in the eyes that Max couldn't help but like.

"Shoot," Max said.

"I knew Ralph was paying a lot for the ball, but I wanted to use some of the money to help Sara out." He sent his sister a self-deprecating look. "I know it's hard on her having an extra person in the house."

"It is not," Sara immediately countered, but Johnny kept talking.

"I want to say something else, too. If I knew where Larry was, I'd track him down myself. I want Ralph to get the rest of his money back. Because the ball was mine and turned out to be fake, it was my fault."

Max noticed that Johnny didn't mention the threat hanging over his head. Neither did he theorize that Larry would feel the same way he did. Larry, who supposedly had disappeared before discovering the ball was fake.

"You got an address for this Ralph? A phone number?" Max asked.

Johnny's gaze met his, then flickered away. "I don't even have a last name. Larry set up the meet. I figured if I needed to contact Ralph, I'd do it through him."

"Then how are you supposed to get the money back to him?"

"He's coming by the coffee shop at noon on Friday."

It was Sunday morning. Max thought about that, conceded it was feasible. "You said you and Larry met with this guy at a restaurant. Did he choose the place or did you?"

"He did. Why?"

"Because if he's a regular, somebody there could know him. What's the name of the restaurant?"

A pause, as though Johnny were trying to dredge it up from his memory. "The Blue Plate, over in Fell's Point. But it didn't seem like anybody there knew him by name."

"It won't hurt to check. After I get a locksmith over here, I'm going to check it out," Max said.

It didn't surprise Max at all when Sara announced she was coming with him.

SARA'S STOMACH CHURNED as she approached the sliding-door entrance of the Blue Plate Diner, but she couldn't attribute her slightly nauseous feeling to the restaurant's garish stainless-steel exterior and electric-blue accents.

Now that Max had met Johnny, she should tell him about her brother's juvenile record. She just wasn't sure she'd be able to.

Max had stuck around her house that morning until the locksmith had arrived, then gone back to his grandparents' house for a shower, shave and change of clothes.

They'd arranged to meet at the diner at one o'clock. It was five minutes before the hour now, but she'd seen Max's car in the parking lot and knew he'd be inside waiting.

He stood half a head taller than the other people

milling about the entrance, making him easy to spot. A little thrill surged through her when he smiled at her, and a desire to be with him replaced her anxiety. She had to consciously stop herself from rushing over to him.

Clean shaven and dressed in chinos, loafers and a terra-cotta canvas shirt, he looked more civilized than the man she'd been dying to kiss last night, but he smelled the same. Like the sandalwood soap he used and Max.

Something else hadn't changed, either. She still wanted him to kiss her.

"Interesting place," Max remarked while they waited for the hostess to seat them. Sara had been so busy noticing Max that only then did she notice the decor.

Hubcaps hung from the walls, some of the customers sat at a stainless-steel counter on swivel stools and waitresses poured sodas from an old-fashioned fountain. The floor was covered in blue and white tile.

"Definitely more retro trendy than old-fashioned," she agreed.

"Look at the clientele." He nodded at the crowd in the busy restaurant. "Older people tend to like Sunday brunches but hardly anybody in here is older than fifty. It doesn't seem like the kind of place Ralph would hang out. Wonder if Johnny could have gotten the restaurant wrong."

At the mention of her brother, Sara's stomach churned all over again. One look at Max and she'd forgotten her resolution to tell him about Johnny. She'd almost forgotten about Ralph.

Now that she remembered, the knowledge that

she was keeping Johnny's past from Max sat like an elephant on her chest.

A young, blond and smiling hostess appeared from the rear of the restaurant and plucked two menus from her stand. Before she'd seated them, she'd already denied ever seeing anybody fitting Ralph's description.

"You might have better luck with Vicki," she said with a broad, dimpled smile. "She'll be your server."

Vicki—just as blond, just as young and just as pleasant—wasn't any more help. She listened attentively while Max relayed the description of Ralph— thick white hair, wire-rimmed glasses, six feet tall, thin—then shook her head.

"You say he's in his seventies? We don't get many senior citizens. I'm not saying he hasn't eaten here, but he doesn't sound familiar."

"He would have been in here Wednesday at lunch time with two younger men, one in his late teens, the other late twenties," Max said. "They were looking at a baseball autographed by Babe Ruth."

"Really? The Babe? Wow. I'd have liked to see that. But, sorry, it still doesn't sound familiar."

After Vicki talked them into trying the house specialty of chicken and dumplings, Max bestowed upon her a smile that lit up his dark eyes and took years off his age.

"Could you do me a favor, Vicki? Could you ask around and see if anybody else knows Ralph? Mention Babe Ruth and the baseball. That might help them remember him."

Vicki's fair cheeks turned a becoming shade of pink. She smiled back at him. "Sure. The same crowd that worked the lunch shift Wednesday is in today. You can count on me."

"Pretty girl," Sara remarked when they were alone in the Naugahyde booth, which was silver with a garish blue lightning stripe across the back. "How old do you think she is? Seventeen? Eighteen?"

"Around there," Max said. "Why?"

Because she was a jealous idiot who wanted to make the point that the waitress was far too young for him, as if a man like Max wouldn't already know that.

"She reminds me of a girl my brother dated in high school," she said to cover her gaffe, then saw an opportunity to turn the conversation to the subject she should be discussing. "Johnny always picked the wholesome types. But then, he's kind of wholesome himself."

"I noticed," Max said, sipping on a tall glass of lemonade that Vicki had brought to the table before taking their orders.

"What did you think of him?"

"Seems like a nice kid."

"He is." Sara realized she was worrying the edge of the blue cloth napkin on her lap and made herself stop. Before she told him about Johnny, maybe she should feel him out a little more. "Did you believe him about the baseball?"

"I didn't *not* believe him. I'm an investigator, Sara. I have to keep an open mind."

It wasn't the definitive answer she wanted.

She studied his face. She could clearly see that he was a handsome man. His features were symmetrical, his skin an attractive shade of bronze, his cheekbones high, his eyes dark and almond shaped. But she couldn't see him.

And because she couldn't, confiding in him would be too risky—even if her heart told her she could trust him.

"I don't know anything about you," she blurted out.

Those beautiful eyes drew questioningly. "Excuse me?"

She composed her thoughts. "I don't know who you are. I don't even know what we're doing here at the diner."

"We're trying to track down Ralph."

"But why?" She asked the question that had nagged her since he'd questioned Johnny that morning. "What does finding this Ralph matter? Isn't it more important to find Larry?"

"An investigation is like a puzzle, Sara. Ralph's one of the pieces. He might say something that will make the other pieces fall in place."

"Is that why you went into law enforcement? Because you liked solving puzzles?"

"I went into law enforcement because my grandparents raised me to believe I should make a difference."

Sara noticed he'd said his grandparents said he *should* make a difference, not *could*. She thought the distinction was important.

"You came to live with them when you were a kid, right? How old were you?"

"Nine." He shifted in the booth. Although he answered easily enough, she sensed he wasn't entirely comfortable with the subject. "I'd been living in Miami with my mother, their daughter, but she couldn't care for me any longer."

"What about your father?"

"He hadn't been in the picture since I was a couple years old."

Sara listened not only to what Max said, but to what he didn't say. What prevented his mother from raising him? Why hadn't his father been in the picture?

Something in his posture prevented her from asking those questions, so she tried an easier one. "What were your grandparents like?"

"Tough but fair," he said. "My grandfather was a family-practice doctor who volunteered his time at a clinic in downtown Baltimore on Saturdays. He was steady, reliable. Somebody you could always count on to do the right thing."

"How about your grandmother?"

"She was no-nonsense, the kind of woman you couldn't get anything past. She made sure I got good grades, stuck to my curfew and knew right from wrong."

But did they love you? Sara wanted to ask. She bit back the question. Of course they'd loved him. They were his grandparents. "They sound like they were hard on you."

"They were, but they were also fair. They spelled out the rules and made sure I followed them. My grandfather was big on actions having consequences."

Sara swallowed. The grandson seemed to have learned that lesson well. But he'd also grown into a good man, a man she couldn't believe would withdraw his help because of Johnny's past mistakes—mistakes her brother had already paid for.

"Which grandparent encouraged you to become a policeman?" she asked, delaying her confession.

"Both," he said. "But my grandfather didn't live to see me become one. He died when I was at the University of Maryland. After I graduated, I took a job with the Baltimore PD so I could be near my grandmother if she needed me. I didn't apply to the FBI until after she died. So that's it."

She tipped her head to the side. "That's what?"

"Everything you could possibly want to know about me."

"Oh, please," she said, managing to smile at him despite her thoughts of Johnny. "That hardly scratches the surface of what I want to know."

But she had confirmed that he was good and honorable and fair-minded—qualities she'd known all along that he possessed.

"There's something I need to tell you about Johnny," she began and took a deep breath.

"Here's your chicken and dumplings." Vicki's bright, cheerful voice interrupted what Sara had been about to say. The waitress set two steaming plates of food in front of them. "You're going to love the food."

She screwed up her cute little nose. "But you're not going to love the news I have about that guy Ralph. I asked the entire staff, and he doesn't sound familiar to anybody. Nobody remembered anything about a baseball, either. Sorry."

"Oops." The cry came from the booth next to them, where a child of about six had knocked over a glass of orange soda. The waitress rushed over to them, pulling out a rag from her apron as she went.

"It's strange that nobody here remembers," Max mused, almost to himself.

"A lot of people go through here," Sara pointed out. "The people who work here can't be expected to remember everybody."

"I mean it's strange that no one remembers the *baseball*. You've seen how friendly the staff is. And you know your brother and Larry. Do they seem like the kind of guys who wouldn't show the waitress an autographed Babe Ruth baseball?"

No, Sara admitted to herself, *they didn't*.

"Now what were you going to tell me about Johnny?" Max asked.

Sara hesitated, second-guessing herself. Max had been openly suspicious of Johnny's story when she'd first relayed it. What if finding out about Johnny's past made him more even more skeptical?

Would he doubt every part of her brother's story? Would he suspect that Johnny had deliberately sent them to the wrong restaurant so they wouldn't hear Ralph's version of the story?

The possibility had occurred to Sara, but she knew Johnny well enough to discount it. Max didn't.

"Sara," Max prodded.

Sara stretched her reluctant lips into a smile. "It was nothing important. I was just going to say that Johnny's really important to me."

SARA WASN'T GOING to tell him about her brother's shoplifting conviction.

For a moment, Max thought she'd been about to come clean. But then Vicki the waitress had arrived bearing their food, and the moment was lost.

He took a forkful of chicken and dumplings, but

barely tasted it as he chewed. Finding out about Johnny had been fairly simple. He'd contacted his FBI partner in El Paso yesterday and had asked him to run quick background checks on both Larry Brunell and Johnny Reynolds.

His partner had called him back an hour ago with the surprising news. Larry Brunell hadn't run into trouble with the law, as Max had suspected. Johnny Reynolds had.

The kid had been convicted of shoplifting in Florida eight months ago, shortly after he'd turned eighteen. The judge fined him, ordered him to perform forty hours of community service and gave him a conditional discharge.

The infraction wasn't serious. But Sara should have told him about it when she'd asked for his help. She should tell him about it now.

Except she wasn't going to.

"Are you sure that's all you were going to say?" he prodded. "You look like something's bothering you."

"You're right," she said. "It's just that I'm…disappointed. I thought, if we could track down Ralph, we might be able to talk him into giving Johnny more time to come up with the money."

Max's own disappointment sat like a ball of lead in his stomach. He debated telling her what he knew about Johnny but kept his mouth shut.

He suspected she feared he'd think her brother was guilty of scamming the old man if she told him about Johnny's prior trouble. But, hell, he'd had his doubts about the whole thing even before he knew anything about her brother.

Not only that, he strongly suspected this wasn't

the restaurant where the three men had met. His hunch was that Johnny didn't want them to find Ralph and hear what had really happened.

But now that Sara was getting to know him better, he wanted her to confide in him. To know in her gut that he'd find Larry because he said he would. If her kid brother was as innocent as she believed—and he hoped that he was—she didn't have anything to worry about.

"Have you always looked out for Johnny?" he asked after a few moments of silence.

She put down her fork, and he studied her while she mulled over his question. In this lighting, her hair looked more golden-brown than blond. Her skin was smooth and clear, her freckles the only thing that kept her complexion from appearing flawless. The light brown color of her eyes was almost the same shade as the root beer in her frosted mug.

"I suppose I always have looked out for him. I'm six years older so he felt like my responsibility. I helped him with his homework, drove him to his practices and listened to his problems."

"Where were your parents?"

"Working. They always had this dream to run an Italian restaurant, which is kind of funny since we're not Italian. They bought a restaurant in Towson when I was fourteen."

"How did that go?"

"It turned a pretty good profit at first but the economy slowed way down the year I graduated from high school."

"Is that when your parents moved to Florida?"

"Oh, no. They were still trying to make the restaurant profitable back then, which was tough even with me helping out full-time."

He put down his fork, too, more interested in her than his food. "You didn't go to college straight from high school?"

"I couldn't. I was working at the restaurant all the time."

"So you didn't always want to be a nurse?"

"Oh, yeah. I did. That's why I enrolled in a community college when things stabilized. But I was still so busy at the restaurant that it took me three years to get a two-year degree."

She said it matter of factly, as though denying her own dream of becoming a nurse to allow her parents to live their dream of running a restaurant hadn't been a sacrifice.

"What happened to the restaurant?"

"My parents got tired of working so hard and sold it. They didn't make a big profit but it was enough for them to retire to Florida and buy a condo. That's where they are now."

"Is that when you started at Johns Hopkins? When they moved?"

"I couldn't. I needed to work for at least a year before I could afford it, even with the loans I took out. I just started a few weeks ago when the fall semester began."

In other words, her parents hadn't helped out. "Why didn't you get any of the money from the sale of the restaurant?"

"It wasn't my restaurant," she said simply, disregarding the sacrifices she'd made for it. "I'll say one thing about working there, though, it made it easy to get a waitressing job."

He frowned. He'd dated a Johns Hopkins student for a couple months when he'd first become a cop, and her life had revolved around medicine.

"But why are you still working at the pub? Shouldn't you have a job in the medical field?"

She wrinkled her nose at him. "Now you sound like my professors. I've only been in nursing school for three weeks but already I hear that all the time, but so far I haven't had time to look for one."

Because she was too preoccupied with her brother and his problems to take care of her own.

A clearer picture of Sara formed in Max's mind, one of a dutiful daughter and sister putting the needs of her family above her own. But it wasn't only her family she looked out for. He thought of Larry, who she'd let live in her house even after they'd broken up. And Trixie, who poured out her problems to Sara but had to squeeze hard for information when something was wrong in Sara's life.

"Where do we go next?" Sara asked.

His eyebrows rose at her choice of pronouns. "*I* need to stop at Larry's apartment building, but *you* don't need to come with me. You're working tonight, right?"

"Yes, but that's not for hours yet."

"Don't you have to study?"

"I can get up early tomorrow morning and look over my notes."

Max sorted out his thoughts. He admired her for trying to help those she cared about, and he understood she was trying to protect her brother by not telling Max about his conviction.

But he wished she'd learn the lesson his grandfather had taught him so well, and that was to let the people in your life make their own mistakes and suffer the consequences.

"Please, Max," she added. "I want to help."

He rubbed the back of his neck. He thought it would be better if she concentrated on her own needs instead of Johnny's. But when she looked at him that way, with her eyes wide and imploring, he couldn't refuse her anything.

"Sure," he said. "As soon as we're through eating, we'll check out Larry's place."

6

SARA NOTICED that Max drove the speed limit through the streets of downtown Baltimore.

Because he'd once worked these very streets, he undoubtedly knew cops didn't have time to ticket drivers who went slightly over the limit. But Max didn't drive thirty-four miles per hour. He didn't drive thirty-one. He drove thirty, the posted speed.

He also braked when the light turned yellow, came to a full halt at stop signs and yielded to pedestrians in crosswalks, all admirable behavior but also all indicators that she'd done the right thing in not telling him about Johnny.

Max followed the rules. She couldn't predict how much tolerance he'd have for those who didn't. Or, in Johnny's case, those who hadn't.

He pulled his rental car to a stop in front of Larry's apartment building, which was in a revitalized section of the city characterized by wide streets and large, shady trees.

She got out of the car and waited for him to join her on the sidewalk. As they walked together past a row of low-cut boxwood hedges and beds of fall flowers in shades of red and yellow, his arm lightly brushed hers. Even though they were in the sun, she felt a shiver of awareness.

Knowing that he always tried to do the right thing hadn't made him less attractive. It had made him more.

Suddenly she wished they weren't looking for Larry or dealing with Johnny. She wished they'd met again by chance and decided to spend time together. Then she wouldn't have to squash her urge to reach for his hand. She'd just grab it.

"You said you'd stopped by Larry's apartment after he disappeared. When was that?" Max asked, the questions bringing her back to reality.

"Friday. I thought he might have told one of his neighbors where he was going, but nobody I talked to knew anything. A couple of them weren't home, though."

The rectangular-shaped apartment building had been cleverly designed so that the fronts of the dwellings faced inward and overlooked a small courtyard. To reach the courtyard and interior staircases, they had to walk through a short corridor that contained banks of mail slots.

Max gestured toward them. "Did you check Larry's slot? If it's empty, he probably asked somebody to pick up his mail."

"I didn't think of that." She walked over to the wall and skimmed her finger down the row of slots until she reached the one corresponding to Larry's apartment number. "It is empty."

"Then let's knock on doors until we find out who has his mail," Max said. "Hopefully that person will have an idea where he is."

"I don't have a clue," the man in the apartment next door to Larry's said a few minutes later.

His name was Frank Ewing. Slim and pale, Frank

had a beak nose, brown hair that had developed male-pattern baldness and a nasal voice. Sara had met him once before, after she'd given in to Larry's pleas and helped him decorate his apartment.

"But you have been picking up Larry's mail? Right, Frank?" Sara said, smiling at him.

Frank smiled back, a brief baring of teeth. He'd cracked open his apartment door a few inches, and the glowing screen of an oversize television was visible beyond his bony shoulder. "Larry asked me to when he stopped by Wednesday."

"After work Wednesday?" Max asked.

"During. I work from home. I buy and sell merchandise on eBay, mostly CDs and DVDs."

"Larry told me you did that," Sara said. "Can you really make a living that way?"

"You'd be amazed. The trick is knowing where to set the opening bid. If it's too low, people think the item's worthless. Too high, they won't bid. I can get a couple thousand for the complete *Star Trek* TV series on DVD. And I once sold a—"

Max didn't let him finish. "So you're saying Larry stopped by in the morning?"

Frank's mouth formed a pout. "No. Right after lunch. I remember, because TNT runs old episodes of the *X-Files* at noon."

"Are you and Larry friends?" Max asked, but Sara already knew the answer. Extroverted Larry didn't have anything in common with this recluse of a man.

"Not really. The only other times we talked, he asked me things about E-Bay. He was interested in my job." Frank sent Max a pointed glare. "Unlike some people."

"Did he say where he was going or when he'd be back?"

"Like I said, he didn't say much of anything." Frank peered up at Max. "Is Larry in trouble? I've seen Sara around here before, but who are you?"

"Max is an FBI agent," Sara supplied.

"An *off-duty* FBI agent," Max clarified.

Frank didn't seem to hear the qualifier. "So you're like a real-life Fox Mulder? Cool. Wait here. I'll get Larry's mail. Maybe it'll yield a clue as to where he went."

After Larry returned with a short stack of mail and disappeared back inside his apartment, Max touched her arm.

"I know you were only trying to be helpful, Sara, but I have to be careful not to mislead anyone into thinking this is an official investigation."

"I'm sorry," Sara said. "I wasn't thinking."

He took his hand away, and she immediately missed its warmth. He walked the few steps to Larry's apartment and she followed him. She was starting to think she'd follow him anywhere.

"Do you want to go in?" Sara asked.

"Sure would. I'd like to make sure there aren't any signs that he left under duress. But again, I'm doing this off the books. So I can't get the super to open the door for us."

"We don't need the super when we have a key." Sara dug into her purse, pulled out her key ring and held up a burnished brass key. "Larry wanted to make sure somebody had a spare."

She'd expected him to smile but instead he frowned. "But why do you have it?"

"Just because we broke up doesn't mean we can't still be friends," she said before inserting the key and unlocking the door.

Sara flicked on lights, revealing an apartment fit for a bachelor. Larry had spent too much for his blocky, modern furniture, but Sara had steered him to a craft store for the brightly hued prints on the wall and a reasonably priced department store for the colorful throw pillows scattered throughout the living room.

She tried to see the place through Max's eyes but wasn't sure she managed it. "Anything look wrong to you?"

"Something feels wrong. If he was planning to be gone for a while, why didn't he turn off the air-conditioning?"

"Larry wouldn't think of something like that," Sara said. "Believe me, I lived with him for a couple of months. He's not the thrifty type."

He leafed through the stack of mail in his hand.

"Any clues in there?" Sara asked.

"Nope. It's mostly bills with some junk mail thrown in," he said before dropping the entire pile on Larry's kitchen table.

Although she already knew the answer, she couldn't stop herself from asking. "You're not going to open it, are you?"

He shook his head.

"But what if one of his credit-card statements includes an advance airline ticket or a first night's deposit in a hotel?"

"That wouldn't change the federal law against

opening another person's mail," he said, his firm tone saying the subject was closed.

They spent a few more minutes looking for clues that weren't there before Max knocked on a few more doors and found out from a few more of Larry's neighbors that they didn't know where he was.

They were passing Frank Ewing's door on the way to Max's car when it swung open. "I just thought of something that might help you," Frank said.

"What's that?" Max asked, clearly skeptical.

"I should have told you this before, but I forgot until just now," Frank said. "You're not the only one who's been asking about Larry. A man came by yesterday, too."

A premonition of danger swept over Sara. Max must have felt it, too, because he positioned himself between Sara and Frank. The threat, however, didn't come from the little man.

"He said he was an old friend of Larry's who was passing through town," Frank continued. "He wanted to know where he might find him."

"Did you tell him what you told us? That you didn't know?" Max asked, but there was an edge to his voice.

"Not exactly. I told him Larry's girlfriend might know," Frank said, his voice a little softer now, as though he sensed he'd done something wrong. He looked past Max to Sara. "I told him your name, Sara, and where you worked."

She felt Max tense beside her. "What did this guy look like?" he asked.

"Tall, dark, muscular. A little on the scary side."

Exactly like the man who'd broken into her apartment.

THE LOCKS ON THE FRONT and back doors were exactly right. High-quality dead bolts with long bolts of hardened steel that would make breaking in through either door exceedingly difficult if not impossible. An alarm system would add extra security, but it wouldn't give Max peace of mind.

Sara wasn't safe here, not when somebody was hunting for Larry and thought she might know where he was.

True, last night's intruder hadn't seemed predisposed to ask questions. He might not even be the same guy who'd visited Larry's apartment building.

But Max wouldn't bet Sara's safety on it. Because if it had been the same guy, he'd been determined enough to find Larry that he'd resorted to breaking and entering.

Things about the break-in that hadn't added up—the lack of anything missing, the fact that the intruder had come at night when someone was likely to be home—suddenly made sense.

Every instinct Max possessed told him Larry was on the run. If Max were running from somebody, he'd take the same precautions Larry had. Not telling his neighbors or friends where he was headed, paying cash for his purchases so as not to leave a paper trail, laying low.

Later Max would have to figure out what Larry had done to warrant such attention, because the reason surely had something to do with why he'd run.

But for now his daunting task was to convince Sara, who'd been looking after herself since she was fourteen, to let him take over the job.

Footsteps on the stairs alerted him that Sara had finished getting ready for work.

He polished off the last of the Oreo he'd found in a cookie jar in the kitchen and went to meet her, stopping in his tracks when bare legs descending the stairs came into view.

They weren't overly long legs, but they had good tone and beautiful curves. The kind of legs that stuck in a man's mind and got him thinking about smoothing his hands up and over them and discovering where they led.

The legs descended first one step, then another, until he could see all of her. She wore a blue-jean miniskirt with a stretchy yellow top that she filled out very nicely. The dream he'd had the night before came rushing back, and he could almost feel his hands cupping her breasts, hear her low, appreciative moans.

Her step faltered, his eyes raised and he faced the damning fact that she'd caught him staring. No use denying it, even though he risked having her guess what he'd been thinking.

"You look pretty," he said.

She smiled, looking uncertain about how to take the compliment. She wore her hair loose today, the yellow of her top highlighting the blonde so that the entire effect was golden.

"Thanks, but I feel like a canary." She touched her top as she came the rest of the way down the steps, stopping just shy of him.

"Canaries everywhere would be proud to hear you say that."

Her eyes dipped away from his, but she didn't stop smiling. "I always wear bright colors when things aren't going the way I want them to. It makes me feel better."

He tipped up her chin with his forefinger and read the worry in her eyes.

"You're concerned about the guy who broke in last night," he stated baldly.

"A little," she admitted, "but I feel better now that new locks are on the doors."

"They won't protect you when you're walking to and from your car."

She released an audible sigh. "I've thought about that. Johnny usually stays up late. I can let him know when I'm leaving work so he can make sure I get home okay."

It was an imperfect plan at best, making Max glad he'd thought to thwart it. "Johnny's going to stay with a friend for a while."

Her eyes rounded. Up close, he could see that they contained little flecks of gold. "When did this happen?"

"At the coffee shop, when you went to the restroom." They'd stopped to ask Johnny if he knew why someone would be looking for Larry. The kid had been appropriately concerned that Larry's problem had come breaking down his sister's door, but he'd professed ignorance.

Johnny's concern had seemed genuine. Max wasn't as sure about the teenager's renewed claim that the Blue Plate Diner was indeed the restaurant where he and Larry had met the elusive Ralph.

"I told your brother I thought the intruder might come back," Max continued. "I told him it would be better if neither of you were here if he did."

"But why would he come back? If he showed up at Larry's apartment, he's not looking for me."

"If it's the same guy—and I should point out we're not one hundred percent certain of that—he could think you know where Larry is. If I hadn't turned up when I did last night, we don't know what he would have done."

"Do you think Larry disappeared because this guy is looking for him?"

"That seems like a good bet," he said.

"What do you think he did?"

"I don't know, but until I do, you can't stay here."

The sun had dipped increasingly lower in the sky since they'd arrived back at her row house. It filtered weakly through the living-room blinds, casting the room in more shadow than light. The shadows played over her face.

"I'm not afraid to stay in my own home," she said, but the tremble in her voice said otherwise.

Max closed the distance between them, placed his hands on her shoulders and stared directly into her eyes. "Listen to me, Sara. It's not safe for you to stay here."

Her chin jutted out stubbornly, but then the fight seemed to go out of her. Maybe it was because of the night that lurked outside the window, growing darker by the second.

"I suppose I could stay with a girlfriend for a couple of days," she said. "I'm sure Trixie would put me up."

"No good. Trixie's no protection."

"You don't know that," Sara objected. "Maybe Trixie's a black belt. Maybe she's like that Tomb

Raider girl, proficient in weaponry. Maybe she's… lethal."

"Is she?"

"Well, no," Sara admitted.

"Then it's settled," he said firmly. "You'll stay with me at my grandparents' house. I'll drive you to and from your classes and work. If this guy's looking for you, he'll have to go through me."

"But…" She gaped at him, clearly not comfortable with the solution. "I don't think it's such a good idea for me to stay with you."

"Why?"

She chewed on her lower lip, drawing his gaze. He wanted to draw that lip into his mouth and soothe her worry. He wanted her to know he'd do anything to keep her safe.

She swallowed. "It's important that I focus on helping Johnny, and you're… distracting."

He couldn't help but smile. He'd sensed that she was attracted to him, but *distracting* had been as close as she'd come to admitting it.

He trailed his slightly callused fingertips down one of her cheeks. "I'm not trying to distract you, Sara. I'm trying to keep you safe."

Her sigh was soft, her breath sweet. "I know I should take exception to that and tell you I can keep myself safe," she said slowly, "but I'll make allowances for you because you're with the FBI. It's in your nature to protect."

He felt the thrill of his victory but didn't gloat. "Then you'll pack a bag?"

"I'll pack a bag," she said.

He watched her disappear up the stairs, his gaze

lingering on her legs. He hadn't dared tell her that his protective instinct was triply keen in her case.

Because if he'd been a quarter of the way in love with her before, he was halfway there now.

THE BAR CROWD THINNED EARLY, as it did every Sunday night when the work week grew imminent. Max had left an hour or so ago with the promise to return for Sara at the end of her shift. Only a few stragglers remained, all of whom occupied the stools surrounding the bar.

Sara wiped up spilled beer from one of the wooden tables and nodded to Trixie, who cleaned up at another table. "No use both of us staying. Why don't you head home?"

Trixie stopped wiping. She usually vibrated with energy but tonight seemed to move in slow motion. "That would be great. I'm whipped. I couldn't sleep last night thinking about what I should do. Pete said he'd go along with whatever I decided."

Sara gave Trixie her full attention. Pete was Trixie's new husband. Trixie's brother had just been awarded full custody of his five-month-old and had asked Trixie to babysit the little girl during the day while he was at work.

"Did you come to a decision?" Sara asked.

Trixie nodded firmly. "I'm going to say no. It isn't fair to either Pete or me if I do this. I love my niece, but she isn't my responsibility. My brother is the one who had unprotected sex with a woman he didn't love."

Sara bit her lip, wondering how much she should say. "But I thought he owned up to that."

"He did. He went to court and fought for his daughter, and I'm proud of him for that." The other waitress's chest heaved up and down. "And I'll let him know I'm willing to help out now and then. But not all the time."

"But if you say no, what will he do?"

"Find a good day-care center, probably. It's not what he wants to do and it'll cost him, but it's the best solution."

Trixie peered at Sara when she didn't respond. "If you were me, you'd help him out, wouldn't you?" She rolled her eyes. "Look who I'm asking. If he were your brother, he'd probably already have moved in with you. Your place is like Grand Central Station."

"It's not as bad as all that," Sara said. "And I'm not you. You have to do what's right for you."

"Thanks for saying that, Sara." Trixie smiled, and Sara smiled back. "Are you sure you're okay with it if I leave?"

"I'm sure. Max is picking me up, so I've got to wait for him."

"What's going on between you two, anyway? Why is he picking you up tonight?"

Sara had already told Trixie about the man who'd broken into her home last night, which made it easier to answer. "He thought it'd be safer if I stayed with him."

Trixie walked closer to Sara, her eyes bright with interest. "Do you and Mr. FBI Guy have something going on?"

Sara felt her face heat and gave the table another swipe in the hopes that Trixie wouldn't notice her blush. "No. Of course not."

"There's no of course about it with a man as hot as that one." Trixie was staring at Sara so intently she felt as though she were under a microscope. "What's wrong with him?"

"Nothing's wrong with him except…" Her voice trailed off, but Trixie was having none of it.

She put her hands on her hips and dug in. "I'm not going away until you tell me. Just as long as you don't tell me that you won't indulge yourself with Hot Stuff because he and Larry are friends."

Sara stopped wiping and frowned. She'd thought of a number of reasons not to get involved with Max but Larry wasn't one of them. They'd been over a long time ago. "Max says he and Larry aren't friends anymore."

"Why not? What happened?"

"I don't know exactly."

"How did they get to be friends anyway? Larry's so happy-go-lucky, and Max is so… not."

"I don't know that, either," Sara said. "But Larry doesn't have anything to do with why I'm hesitating to get involved with Max."

"What is it then?" she demanded.

"It's just that he's so…principled." Sara searched for a way to explain something that sounded so irrational. "I know that's a good thing. It's even part of what makes Max so attractive. But I worry that he sees the world in black and white, with no gray in between."

"You're worried that he'll turn Johnny over to the police if he finds out he's guilty?"

"Exactly."

"He might surprise you, honey. A guy doesn't always act the way you think he will when he's crazy about a woman." She put a hand to her mouth. "Oh, look at that. I told him I'd let him tell you but I went and blurted it out anyway."

"He told you he was crazy about me?"

"I guessed, and he didn't deny it. That's as good as an admission in my book." Trixie reached out and hugged her. "Don't look so worried, Sara. It's a good thing when you've got a hot guy with principles lusting after you."

Trixie gave a wave, then headed for the door.

Sara's heartbeat quickened, and she admitted some truths to herself. She should have found Max's protective behavior annoying, but it had been so long since anyone had looked out for her that he filled a need she hadn't even known she had.

But that wasn't the reason for her accelerated heartbeat. Neither was fear at staying in the same house as Max.

Her heart beat hard with anticipation because she could hardly wait to be alone with him.

MAX KEPT SARA BEHIND HIM while he stepped from the dark night into the foyer, but the precaution was unnecessary. Sara's home had brimmed with menace the night before, but tonight his grandparents' house was still and empty.

His memory played a trick on him, rewinding to one of the many nights he'd come home late when he was a teenager. He saw his grandmother descending the stairs, dressed in a cotton nightgown and the bright pink robe that made her look like an aging flamingo. She crossed her arms over her chest, silently waiting for Max to explain why he was late.

Max blinked. Just like that, his grandmother was gone.

He waited for the overwhelming feeling of abandonment to sweep over him, as it had the other times he'd entered the house, but it didn't come.

And suddenly he knew the reason. Because he wasn't alone. Sara was with him. Sara, who had started to fill a barren place in his heart he hadn't known was empty.

She pulled the door closed behind them and he gently moved her aside so he could lock it. He wasn't leaving anything to chance.

During the drive from the Rusty Nail, he'd filled her in on how he'd spent his night. When nobody suspicious had turned up at Rusty's, he'd checked out a nearby bar Larry sometimes frequented on his nights off.

A few of the people there knew Larry, including a pretty bartender who said he'd made a date with her that past weekend and then stood her up. But again the story was the same. Nobody knew where he'd gone or where he might be.

"I didn't ask how you knew Larry hung out at that bar," Sara remarked as she moved deeper into the house.

"Almost all the guys Larry and I hung out with in high school are married. I figured he probably spent the most time with the guy who was still single and asked him."

"Jimmy Howerton," Sara supplied the name, once more demonstrating an intimate knowledge of Larry's life.

Something had been gnawing at him since she'd re-entered his life, and he couldn't hold back the question any longer. "Are you sure things between you and Larry are over?"

Her head pivoted, her expression surprised. "Of course I'm sure. Why do you ask?"

"You and Larry broke up months before he moved into that apartment, right?"

"That's right," she confirmed.

"Then why does Frank Ewing still think you're Larry's girlfriend?"

"I don't know. My guess is because he saw me with Larry and made a bad assumption."

"You're not still in love with Larry?"

"I was never in love with Larry."

Max knew he didn't have a right to interrogate her like this but couldn't stop the questions from coming. "Then why did you let him stay with you after you broke up?"

"Because he needed a place to live," Sara said simply. "And I like him."

"You still feel that way? Even when it seems like he talked your brother into passing off a fake Babe Ruth autograph as genuine?"

"That's your opinion," Sara said, bristling. "I don't think it happened that way."

"Okay, then here's another question for you. Why would you still have such a high opinion of Larry after somebody broke into your place looking for him?"

"I never said I had a high opinion of him. I know he has faults. I said I liked him. And it's hardly his fault somebody broke into my house."

"It sure as hell isn't yours." Max rubbed the back of his neck. "I would have thought you'd see through him by now."

"Let me ask you something," Sara said. "Why are you always so willing to believe the worst of Larry?"

Max shoved his fingers through his hair, irritated that she kept sticking up for the guy. "Maybe because I know him better than you do."

"You mean *knew* him. You said yourself you haven't seen or talked to him in more than a year."

"I doubt he's changed that much." Max sighed at the sharp look she sent him, but maybe it was time she knew what kind of man Larry really was. "You really want to hear this story?"

"I really want to hear it."

Suddenly weary, he looked for a place to get off his feet. The stairs were closest so he sat on one of the bottom steps. After a moment's hesitation, Sara joined him. Their shoulders were inches apart, but the staircase was wide enough that their bodies didn't touch.

"When we came into the house tonight," Max began, "I remembered how my grandmother used to wait up for me when I stayed out past curfew."

"I can't picture you as a rebellious teenager," Sara said.

He rubbed his lower face, which felt bristly against his fingers, and realized it was very late. He'd had a five o'clock shadow for almost nine hours. "I wasn't particularly rebellious. But like I told you before, my grandparents were strict. They didn't trust some of the friends I hung out with."

Understanding dawned in her eyes. "You're talking about Larry, aren't you?"

"Yeah, I am," he said softly.

"But why? What was so terrible about him?"

"Larry tended to get in trouble. Not major trouble,

but bad enough. He got suspended for cheating on a test, got picked up for shoplifting, that kind of thing." He watched her carefully when he mentioned shoplifting, but she didn't react.

"My grandparents wanted me to stay away from Larry," he continued, "but I couldn't cut all ties with him, not after what he did for me when I was a kid."

"What did he do?"

"Prevented my life from becoming a living hell, basically. If not for Larry, I'd have been miserable when I came to live with my grandparents." He'd started out intending to tell her about Larry, but realized the story was mostly about himself. It was a story he'd never told another woman, but found he wanted to share with Sara. "I was small for my age and my English wasn't good so the other kids teased me."

"You couldn't speak English?" He heard the surprise in her voice. "But I thought you were nine when you came to Maryland."

"I was. And I could speak English, just not well." He gazed down at his hands, finding it easier to tell the story when he didn't look at her. "In the Little Havana section of Miami, where I came from, the primary language is Spanish. Even at school, all the teachers are bilingual. My attendance record wasn't very good so whenever I couldn't make myself understood, I slipped back into Spanish."

"But didn't your mother grow up here in Maryland?"

"In this very house. But she got pregnant with me when she was seventeen and ran off to Miami with my father, who's Cuban. He wanted me to grow up speaking Spanish."

"I'd never have guessed your first language was

Spanish," she said softly. "You don't have even the trace of an accent."

"That's because my grandparents got me tutors and stressed they wanted me to sound like an American. My full name is Diego Maxwell Dolinger. They dropped the Diego and started calling me Max."

He glanced at her, expecting that she'd have trouble understanding. She'd grown up with two parents in the comfortable world of suburbia. But her eyes had softened.

"It must have been difficult for you to leave all that you'd known and come to what was essentially another culture."

"It would have been worse if not for Larry."

Max could still picture the moment he and Larry had become friends. Max had been passing through the playground, relieved that the other children had largely moved from teasing him to ignoring him. He'd told himself he didn't care.

"Hey, Dolinger, come over here," Larry had yelled. "We're playing pickup football and I picked you."

He'd hardly believed he'd heard correctly. Although Larry had never started the name calling, he'd laughed along with the rest of the boys. Still, Larry hadn't needed to ask him twice.

Max had helped Larry's team win that playground game and many more afterward. He'd suspected the other boy had reached out after seeing Max fire a football through an old tire he'd suspended from a tree limb. But the reason hardly mattered.

Max was in, his problems with his classmates a thing of the past.

"Larry befriended me," Max said simply, "and pretty soon the other kids accepted me, too."

"And you and Larry stayed friends all through high school?"

"Friends, not close friends. But we did run in the same crowd."

"That would explain why I'd never seen you until Kevin Carmichael's wedding," she mused. "But if you and Larry had remained friendly for that long, why aren't you friends now?"

Max looked into her face, watching the curiosity that had bloomed there. When he'd begun this story, he hadn't intended to tell her the way it ended. But he didn't want to hold anything back from her.

He took a deep breath, then plunged ahead, "Larry figured out that I wanted you."

7

SARA HAD HEARD of other people being shocked speechless, but it had never happened to her. Until this moment. She felt her mouth drop open, her vocal chords freeze, her heart cease normal activity and begin a slow thump.

She was the reason Max and Larry were no longer friends.

"It happened at the wedding," Max continued. "Larry asked why I kept looking at you. I told the truth, that I thought you were gorgeous. He told me to stay the hell away from you. End of friendship. End of story."

She tried to process the information. It explained so much. The way Larry had changed the subject whenever she'd brought up Max's name. The warning Kevin had issued not to bother asking Max about Larry. The reason Max had said he'd help her.

"So you stayed away," she whispered.

"I stayed away," he confirmed, "but not for the reasons Larry thought I did. I didn't want to create a scene at Kevin's wedding. And, besides—"

"You'd never try to steal a friend's girl," she finished for him.

"That's right," he said, "but how did you know I was going to say that?"

"I know because that's the kind of man you are."

His laugh sounded self-deprecating. "I'm not as noble as you think I am. Larry didn't have it so wrong. I wouldn't have made a move on you, but I sure wanted to." He puffed his cheeks with air, let them deflate. "Since I'm telling you my secrets, I might as well share another one."

She held her breath. He didn't touch her but she felt his breath on her cheek, smelled the outdoors on his shirt, saw the intensity in his dark eyes.

"I still want to make a move on you."

His deep voice was low and smoky. A lover's voice. But despite his declaration, he didn't move other than the rise and fall of his chest. And she understood.

"But you won't," she said, "because you told me your help doesn't have strings attached."

"It doesn't."

She reached out and touched her fingertips to his lips. It seemed like she'd been wanting to touch him forever. "Would it make a difference if I told you I wanted you to kiss me?"

His lips curved upward again, and he touched her cheek with surprisingly gentle fingers. His eyes went darker than the moonless night outside the door, and his voice was whisper soft.

"Oh, yeah," he said.

He inched closer so that his lips were no more than a finger's width from hers. Her entire body yielded at the sound of his husky, caressing voice. Her breath caught. Her heart pounded.

"I do," she whispered.

Max kissed her fingertips first. Then his mouth closed over hers, his lips soft and coaxing. He kissed the center of her mouth, then the sides, before tracing his tongue lightly over her lips.

One of his hands trailed down her arm, just her arm, leaving goose bumps in its wake. The other hand stroked her cheek as he kissed her, a gesture so sweet her chest ached.

When had she started to fall for him? Had it been when he'd come charging to her rescue? Or in the park when he'd explained that he'd offered his help without expecting anything in return? Or had it dated back to the wedding when she'd watched the way he'd conducted himself and had liked what she'd seen?

She couldn't pinpoint the moment, but she did know that it was too hard to keep fighting the attraction.

She sank into the kiss, opening her mouth, inviting him in. His tongue dipped and stroked the roof of her mouth, the tip of her tongue. Liquid heat flared inside her.

There was none of the hesitancy that often accompanied a first kiss, none of the self-consciousness. She wound her arms around his neck, tangling her fingers in his hair, trying to get closer.

His hand moved lower, running over the muscles of her back before bringing her soft chest flush against the hardness of his. Her eyes were closed, but she saw colors. Vivid colors, like the ones she wore to cheer herself up.

He moved restlessly against her, and her back came up against the unforgiving ledge of a wooden step. She winced, a movement he couldn't miss. He drew back a few inches, regarding her quizzically.

"The stairs," she said. "They're hard."

Just like that, they reached a turning point in their relationship. She knew it as well as he did. The pad of his forefinger traced her lower lip, which was still moist from his kisses. She shivered with renewed awareness.

"You could come upstairs with me."

She closed her eyes and her head spun. It had been so easy to kiss him when she hadn't thought beyond the moment, but his invitation forced her to consider whether going to bed with him would be wise.

Too much was happening too quickly. How could she trust that sleeping with Max would be the right thing to do when her head was full of worry about Johnny and questions about Larry?

She opened her eyes, read the hope in his and almost wished she were the type of woman who slept around.

"I can't go to bed with you, Max." She drew a breath. "I won't pretend I don't want to, but making love isn't something I do lightly. And there's a lot on my mind right now for me to know about whether this is right."

His hand dropped from her mouth and he edged away so that he no longer touched her. His breathing was slightly uneven, his skin flushed, his arousal impossible to hide.

"Did it ever occur to you that you're so involved in everybody else's life that you don't have time to live your own?"

She shook her head, dismayed at his question. But

maybe the fact that he'd asked was a sign that not sleeping with him had been the right decision. She didn't know how not to be involved with the people she cared about.

If she slept with Max, he'd catapult to the top of her VIP list. She knew how she operated. She didn't have flings, she had relationships. She'd need to have him in her life, and she feared Max was too self-sufficient to need anyone.

"I get involved, Max," she said, trying to explain. "That is how I live my life."

"But you're not going to let yourself get involved with me?" he asked, then waved a hand. "No, don't answer that. I don't want you to think I'd try to talk you into sleeping with me. I wouldn't do that. Not after you already said no."

He looked so earnest that desire rose up and clogged her throat. It was a moment before she could speak. "Thank you," she finally said.

He nodded. "You can take the first room on the right. That's the guest room. There are clean sheets in the closet. I can help you put them on the bed."

"No. I'll do it." She couldn't risk spending one more moment in his presence, not when she already regretted her decision. She got to her feet, not surprised that her legs felt shaky. Her entire body felt that way. "Good night, Max."

She slowly climbed the steps, each one taking her farther away from the man she desperately wanted.

"Sara."

She stopped, but didn't turn around. His soft, low voice drifted up the stairs.

"Could I have talked you into sleeping with me?"

She smiled at the wistful tone of his voice, not having the heart to disappoint him further by admitting that it wouldn't have taken much persuasion.

"That," she said, "is something you'll just have to wonder about."

His soft laughter followed her up the stairs.

MAX DRUMMED HIS FINGERS on the steering wheel as he fought the Monday morning traffic, thinking about whether he could have talked Sara into sharing his bed the night before.

She sat in the passenger seat, sipping on a cup of cappuccino they'd picked up before getting on the interstate en route to nursing school. He slid a glance at her, only to find her staring at him.

She looked away first, but not before their eyes locked and he felt attraction humming in the air.

This new, heightened awareness convinced him that last night he could have uttered some pretty words, swept her into his arms and kissed her until she didn't remember what her objections were or even that she'd had any.

Frustration was on him like a cold, biting wind. Even though he'd ached for her last night and ached for her still, he'd done the right thing by resisting the urge to change her mind.

His resolve to let Sara know that he was trustworthy was even stronger than his desire to make love to her.

It was essential that she understand he hadn't tricked her into staying with him to get her into bed. Just as he hadn't offered to find Larry because he expected something in return.

If he could prove he was a man of his word, she might eventually grow to trust him and not only with full disclosure about her brother's past. The stakes were already higher than that.

He wanted her to trust him with her heart.

He took the exit for downtown Baltimore, then gave in to temptation and looked at her again. She folded, unfolded and refolded the hands in her lap before her eyes met his.

"Why do you keep looking at me like that?" she asked.

He swung his gaze back to the road, safely merging into traffic that had begun to thin slightly. At nearly ten o'clock, the worst of the rush hour had passed. Then he glanced at her again. "Like what?"

She swallowed. "Like you want to kiss me."

He hadn't expected her to state it so baldly but was encouraged that she had. It meant he wasn't the only one who couldn't get last night out of his mind.

"Because I do," he stated.

"But you won't."

"Not until you let me know you want me to."

She broke eye contact, looking out the passenger window at rows of warehouses that had been converted into trendy restaurants and shops. He thought he heard her sigh.

They didn't talk again until he pulled to the curb on North Wolfe Street in front of the five-story Anne M. Pinkard Building that housed the Johns Hopkins school of nursing.

"Your classes end at five and your shift at the bar begins at six, right?" he asked after he'd put his car in park.

"That's right."

"I'll meet you inside the building beside the security desk, drive you to your house so you can change clothes and drop you at the pub."

She didn't have to ask how he planned to spend his day. He'd already told her he meant to canvass some of Larry's regular hangouts for leads on where he might have gone.

Her hand reached for the door handle, then froze there. The sun hit her full in the face when she turned back to him. "I really appreciate all you're doing for me and Johnny, Max. It means a lot."

She flashed him a smile, slipped out of the car and shut the door. He stayed at the curb, watching her until she disappeared into the building.

Then he put his car in gear and drove to the salon where Larry got his hair cut. Wedged between a bakery and a Chinese restaurant on a busy commercial street, it wasn't the trendiest of salons. But to Max, it was trendy enough. He got his hair cut at a barbershop.

"A friend of mine recommended I come here. Name of Larry Brunell," he told the young girl at the desk. Her hair was straight, shiny and so long it looked like it hadn't been cut in years. Not the best advertisement for a salon.

"Yeah, I know Larry," she said, flipping the long hair behind her ears. "Short on the sides, longer on top, don't shave off the sideburns."

"You cut his hair?'

"No, Kim does." She nodded at a lovely Asian woman in her forties who probably wasn't taller than five feet three even with her stacked heels. "I just pay attention."

Kim used an economy of motion to put tiny rollers into a young woman's hair while she chatted nonstop. This didn't look like the best time for Max to ask her questions.

"Does Kim have any openings today?" he asked on a flash of inspiration.

The girl skimmed a very long nail down the appointment book, then looked up at him.

"You're in luck. You usually have to book her weeks in advance but sometimes things open up on Mondays. She has a cancellation today at two. Do you want it?"

It was eleven o'clock now, but he could keep busy until then checking out some of the other places on Sara's list. The deli that served Larry's favorite Reuben sandwich. The bakery where he bought chocolate éclairs. The liquor store where he picked up bottles of merlot.

Max was back at the shop at two o'clock sharp, no closer to finding Larry than he'd been three hours earlier. At five minutes past two, he was in the cushioned swivel chair at Kim's station, his hair shampooed and ready for a cut. At ten minutes past, Kim was talking about Larry as she snipped away.

"Larry, he's a good customer," she said. "He was in here last week."

"What day?"

"Tuesday, I think."

Larry and Johnny had sold the ball with the fake autograph on Wednesday. He'd disappeared on Thursday. Today was Monday.

"Did he say anything to you about taking a trip?"

She thought a minute. "No, nothing."

"Did Larry seem worried about anything?"

"That Larry, he's always worried about something." She kept cutting, not bothering to ask why Max wanted to know. "That guy always looks like a million bucks, but the way he talks you'd think he didn't have a dime."

"So he complains about money?"

"Oh, yeah. Honey, you wouldn't believe the things people tell their hairdressers. I hear so many confessions sometimes I feel like a priest."

"What did Larry have to confess about?"

Kim laughed and made another snip. "I can't tell you that, honey. What customers say to Kim, remains with Kim. For all I know, you're Sara's new boyfriend."

"You know Sara?"

"Never seen her before. But I know Larry messed up so bad with that girl, he'll have a hard time getting her back. Why you asking all these questions, anyway?"

Unless he came clean, the verbal well would run dry. He thought about how to phrase his statement so that Kim would be concerned but not panicked.

"Larry left town abruptly, and nobody knows where he is. I'm trying to track him down to make sure he's okay."

Kim was silent for a few moments as she continued to shape his hair.

"That Larry, he knows how to look out for number one," she said. "That's probably why he left town."

"If you know something that would help me find him, Kim, I'd appreciate it if you told me."

She leaned close, so nobody in the shop could overhear. "I think maybe you should talk to Darryl."

"You got a last name for this Darryl or a place I can find him?"

She shook her head. "All I know is the name. And that Larry owes Darryl money."

"Who is Darryl?"

"That I couldn't tell you, honey. You're going to have to figure out that one for yourself."

DARRYL COULD HAVE BEEN a ghost for all the traces Max found of him.

Sara wasn't familiar with the name. When he checked that night with the other employees at Rusty's, they all said they'd never heard of Darryl, either. Neither had anyone at the other bar where Larry sometimes hung out.

Nobody, it seemed, knew anybody named Darryl.

Then again, nobody knew anything about the guy who'd been staring at Sara the other night, either.

Max leaned forward on his bar stool and gestured to attract the bartender's attention. With sun-bleached blond hair and a deep tan, he looked more like a college frat boy than a bartender. And that's what he was, part of the time. When Max had talked to him earlier about Larry, he'd mentioned he was bartending to help pay for college. His name was Tim.

"You need another already?" Tim picked up a bottle of tonic water and grinned. "Sure you can handle it?"

"I can drink anybody under the table when it comes to this stuff," Max said, lifting a glass that was still three-quarters full of tonic water. "But what I need is the answer to another question."

"Shoot." Tim flashed a set of blinding-white teeth.

GET FREE BOOKS and a FREE GIFT WHEN YOU PLAY THE...

Lucky 7

SLOT MACHINE GAME!

Just scratch off the silver box with a coin. Then check below to see the gifts you get!

YES! I have scratched off the silver box. Please send me the 2 free Harlequin Blaze™ books and gift for which I qualify. I understand I am under no obligation to purchase any books, as explained on the back of this card.

350 HDL D7W4   **150 HDL D7XJ**

FIRST NAME   LAST NAME

ADDRESS

APT.#   CITY

STATE / PROV.   ZIP / POSTAL CODE

7	7	7	**Worth TWO FREE BOOKS plus a BONUS Mystery Gift!**
🍒	🍒	🍒	**Worth TWO FREE BOOKS!**
♣	♣	♣	**Worth ONE FREE BOOK!**
🔔	🔔	🍒	**TRY AGAIN!**

www.eHarlequin.com

(H-B-04/05)

Offer limited to one per household and not valid to current Harlequin Blaze™ subscribers. All orders subject to approval.

© 2000 HARLEQUIN ENTERPRISES LTD. ® and TM are trademarks owned and used by the trademark owner and/or its licensee.

DETACH AND MAIL CARD TODAY!

The Harlequin Reader Service® — Here's how it works:

Accepting your 2 free books and gift places you under no obligation to buy anything. You may keep the books and gift and return the shipping statement marked "cancel." If you do not cancel, about a month later we'll send you 4 additional books and bill you just $3.99 each in the U.S., or $4.47 each in Canada, plus 25¢ shipping & handling per book and applicable taxes if any.* That's the complete price and — compared to cover prices of $4.75 each in the U.S. and $5.75 each in Canada — it's quite a bargain! You may cancel at any time, but if you choose to continue, every month we'll send you 4 more books, which you may either purchase at the discount price or return to us and cancel your subscription.

*Terms and prices subject to change without notice. Sales tax applicable in N.Y. Canadian residents will be charged applicable provincial taxes and GST. Credit or debit balances in a customer's account(s) may be offset by any other outstanding balance owed by or to the customer.

If offer card is missing write to: Harlequin Reader Service, 3010 Walden Ave., P.O. Box 1867, Buffalo NY 14240-1867

NO POSTAGE
NECESSARY
IF MAILED
IN THE
UNITED STATES

BUSINESS REPLY MAIL
FIRST-CLASS MAIL   PERMIT NO. 717-003   BUFFALO, NY

POSTAGE WILL BE PAID BY ADDRESSEE

HARLEQUIN READER SERVICE
3010 WALDEN AVE
PO BOX 1867
BUFFALO NY 14240-9952

"You ever see a guy in here about five-six, two hundred pounds, looks like he could be a body-builder?" Max remembered the nickname Trixie had given him. "Sort of like a younger, miniature Arnold Schwarzenegger."

"Sure. He was in here late last week playing pool."

"That's him." Max tried to keep from sounding too eager. "Know anything about him?"

"I heard some things." Tim looked right, then left, before bringing his head close to Max's and lowering his voice. "He looks like the muscle for a loan shark, but I hear he *is* the loan shark."

Max's pulse pounded. Could Darryl and the muscleman be one and the same? If Larry was indebted to a loan shark, that would explain why he'd talked Johnny into selling the baseball and splitting the profits. If Larry hadn't completely repaid his debt, it could even explain why he was on the lam and why someone was looking for him. "Who told you that?"

"I don't remember, exactly. Why? You think that guy has something to do with Larry being gone?"

Max didn't answer while he turned over possibilities. "You ever get a sense that Larry was gambling?"

Tim shrugged. "Could be. Larry never had cash. But if you want to know for sure, ask Sara."

Max nodded, noting that yet another source was aware that Larry had a lingering relationship with Sara.

"Thanks." Max rose from the bar stool and scanned the bar for Sara. He found her immediately. With her fair-colored hair and the light that seemed to glow from within, she stood out like a beacon.

She bent forward to deliver a drink, throwing the outline of her breasts into focus. She laughed at something the customer said, lighting up her pretty face and making Max wish she'd look at him that way.

She turned away from the table, the smile still on her lips. Their gazes locked and electricity hummed in the air between them.

He felt the corners of his own mouth lift and advanced across the bar to meet her halfway. Her smile seemed to hold a promise. Had she stopped fighting the inevitable?

"Your hair's really short," she said. "Even for an FBI agent."

So much for reading too much into a look, Max thought.

"I already told you," he said. "Larry's hairdresser was so busy, I couldn't talk to her unless I became a customer."

"I didn't say I didn't like it." She reached out and touched the short strands. "I said it was short."

Their gazes locked again and he revised his opinion. Maybe he hadn't read too much into that slow, sexy look.

"Is there somewhere we can talk?" he asked.

She gazed around the bar, which was filling up even though it was Monday evening.

"Trixie's running late so I can't spare more than a couple minutes." She nodded toward a table near the back wall. "Why don't we talk back there? That way I'll be available if I'm needed."

He watched the gentle sway of her hips as he followed her to the table. Desire flared but turned to concern when she got off her feet and a sigh escaped her lips. Waitressing was hard work for anyone, but especially for a full-time nursing student who'd been on the go since ten that morning and was filling in for the bar manager. He wondered if she ever took a night off.

Their gazes locked and again he felt that indefinable pull that was only partly sexual. Even if she never set foot in his bedroom, he'd care what happened to her.

"You really should look for that other job," he said. "Your life might get easier if you didn't have to waitress."

"I've thought of that, and I plan to do it when all this is over. But keeping my brother out of jail is what's most important to me right now."

Only if your brother deserves to stay out of jail, Max thought but swallowed the potentially inciting words and went straight to his point.

"I need to know if Larry could have been gambling."

"Sure, it's possible," she said. "We both know he has faults. Gambling could have been one of them. Why do you ask?"

"That guy Darryl, I think he might be a loan shark."

"So what you're really asking is whether I think Larry is on the run because he racked up gambling debts he couldn't pay."

"Yeah," Max admitted. "That's what I'm really asking."

She took her time in answering. "I think Larry's too smart for that. I can see him borrowing money, but not from somebody who would break his legs if he didn't pay."

She focused on something beyond his shoulder. "It's getting busier, and somebody over there's signaling for me. I'd love to stay here with you, but I'd better go."

She flashed him a smile, got up and left. Max stayed at the table after she'd gone. He was watching her take a drink order when he caught a movement out of the corner of his eye. Tim, waving his arms. The bartender pointed to the entrance of the bar and Max spotted the alleged loan shark.

Luckily, the man didn't appear to notice Tim's wild hand gestures. Unluckily, that was probably because he was staring at Sara.

She smiled broadly as she took orders from a trio of middle-aged guys wearing sneakers and gym shorts who looked like they'd been playing basketball. Max usually suspected that waitresses who smiled that way were angling for a big tip, but Sara's smile appeared genuine.

They guy in question stopped at the bar, signaled for the bartender and placed an order. He propped his hip against the bar while he waited, his body angled to give him a better view of Sara. After Tim delivered a bottle of lager, he sauntered over to his usual place at the back of the pub.

Four rowdy young guys and a couple of pretty young women in their twenties occupied the pool tables, but the man barely glanced at them. He leaned negligently against a wall, sipping his beer, his eyes never straying from Sara.

Enough was enough.

Leaving his tonic water on the table, Max rose and didn't stop walking until he stood next to the muscleman. The man glanced up, but otherwise didn't acknowledge him.

Max watched one of the pool players bank the four-ball into the corner pocket, then spoke. "I heard you were the guy to talk to about a cash advance."

The other man's gaze slid to his, his small eyes hard with suspicion. "Who the hell told you that?"

"Doesn't matter who told me. What matters is if it's true."

"It's not," he retorted with heat.

Max studied the other man for one of the tells that would brand him as a liar—a change in eye contact, nervous movements of the feet and legs, a hand reaching to cover part of the face. He didn't do any of those things.

"Just 'cause I don't look like a legitimate business-man doesn't mean I'm not," he added sourly.

"Oh, yeah. What do you do?"

"I run a gym," he said, and Max heard pride in his voice. "The Ten Count."

Max remembered the name from his days as a pa-trol cop. He'd never been there himself but fellow of-ficers had once or twice been called to the gym to break up fights that had continued beyond the ring.

"You train boxers," Max stated.

"That's right. I'm in the business of developing tal-ent, not making loans." He raised a bushy black eye-brow. "You a cop or something?"

"Or something," Max said. "I'm looking for a guy by the name of Larry Brunell. I thought you might know where he is."

"Never heard of him." The man met Max's gaze head-on, but that didn't mean he told the truth. Ac-complished liars knew eye contact made them seem more convincing.

Max nodded at Sara. "How about her? Do you know her?"

"The waitress?" His already small eyes narrowed. His breath smelled of beer. "There's no law against looking at a pretty girl."

"That's true," Max said, leaning down so his face was closer to the man's. "But if something happens to that girl, I'll know where to look."

The man's lips developed an ugly curl, and he pushed away from the wall. "You're way off base, man. I don't care who you are. I'm not gonna stay here and let you bust my chops."

Max let him get two steps before he called, "Hey, Darryl."

When the man didn't respond, Max caught up to him and tapped him on the shoulder. "I'm talking to you, Darryl."

"My name's not Darryl, asshole," he said sneering.

He shouldered through the crowd, looking like he wanted to put as much distance as possible between himself and Max.

"Hey, are you looking for Darryl?" The question came from the tallest and thinnest of the four men playing pool. He nodded toward the very rear of the bar. "Back there."

The only person in the vicinity was big-boned, pleasant-faced and dark-haired and drinking a tall glass of Guinness Stout. Darryl, it seemed, was a woman.

Unlike the gym owner, she didn't dodge his questions. Yes, she knew Larry. Yes, she'd lent him money. And yes, he'd owed her big.

"Did you know Larry was missing?" Max asked.

"Isn't any of my business," she said.

"It is if he's running because you threatened him with violence if he didn't pay you back."

Her dark eyebrows drew together. "Who said he didn't pay me back?"

"You did," Max said. "Just now."

"I said he *owed* me, not that he *owes* me." She took a swig of Stout straight from the bottle, then set it back down with a thump. "He paid me back every red cent last week."

8

SARA TOSSED, TURNED and finally gave up on sleep. Sitting up on the soft queen-size mattress, she shoved her hair back from her face and swung her legs out of bed.

The luminescent numbers on the bedside alarm clock showed it was just past 3:00 a.m.

Although fatigue weighed down her limbs, her mind wouldn't shut off. Thoughts of Larry, the loan shark, Johnny, the baseball with the fake autograph and fifteen thousand dollars swirled through her head until she couldn't stand it anymore.

If she were home, she'd read until her eyes went glassy but the only book she'd brought with her was a textbook for her class about the context of nursing in the health-care system. Well, reading that would do the trick.

She switched on the bedside light, covering her eyes and squinting against the sudden brightness, then remembered she'd left the textbook downstairs. Groaning, she located her faithful yellow robe, pulled it on and went in search of her textbook.

She expected the narrow upstairs hallway to be dark, but a light shone from a partially open door. It wasn't the bedroom Max was sleeping in, but a larger room, farther down the hall.

Walking silently on bare feet to the staircase, she heard rustling sounds coming from the room. She padded toward the light, which illuminated what had surely been his grandparents' room.

An old-fashioned white bedspread in the George Washington style covered a four-poster mahogany bed. White doilies decorated the surfaces of the matching dressers and nightstands, and lacy full-length curtains hung from the windows. Max crouched on his knees in front of a roll-top desk, a garbage bag on one side of him, a box on the other.

"Couldn't sleep?" He didn't look over his shoulder until after he'd spoken. Stubble showed on his lower face, and he wore a faded University of Maryland T-shirt and lightweight gray sweatpants.

"How did you know I was here?" she asked.

Those dark eyes seemed to pin her in place. "I felt you."

Her body filled with a heavy languor, making it difficult to move. She didn't have to ask what he meant. When she'd gone to sleep tonight, knowing that he was only a few doors down the hall, she'd felt him, too.

"I keep worrying about the consequences for Johnny if Larry already spent the money," she said, partly to deflect the awareness that had sprung between them and partly because it was true.

"Will it help if I tell you again that your brother doesn't have anything to worry about if he's innocent? When I find Larry, he can corroborate Johnny's story."

When he'd told her the same thing on the drive from the pub, she'd nearly confided that Johnny had a juvenile record that would work against his believability. Again, she wanted to tell him. Again, she didn't.

"I don't think anything's going to help me sleep except maybe my textbook," she said. "I got up because I left it downstairs. Couldn't you sleep, either?"

"I never went to bed," he said. "The realtor's selling the house furnished and I'm leaving the linens and kitchen supplies, but I haven't finished going through my grandparents' personal things."

She crossed the room to his side, immediately contrite. "It's my fault you don't have more time for this. I should help you."

"Thanks," he said, a sigh in his voice, "but this is something I have to do myself."

No matter how broad his shoulders, Sara thought, the task had to weigh heavily on him. She glanced into the box and noticed Max had kept little for himself: a few pieces of his grandmother's jewelry, his grandfather's war medals, old photos.

The top one captured her attention, and she dropped to her knees beside him and picked it up. "Is this you and your grandparents?"

Max glanced at the photo. "Yeah. That was taken the week I came to live with them."

He stood between the two adults, a small, thin boy with a shock of black hair, his dark eyes not meeting the camera, his body language defensive.

Nobody in the photo touched, although Max's austere-looking grandmother looked down at him bemusedly. His grandfather was as pale as Max was dark, but his erect posture and the air of confidence he projected reminded Sara of his grown-up grandson.

Neither of his grandparents seemed like particularly warm people. How hard it must have been for

the young Max to suddenly find himself living
with them.

"What happened to your parents, Max?" She
voiced the question she'd been reluctant to ask in the
diner. "Why didn't they raise you?"

He was silent for so long that she added, "Please
tell me, Max. I want to know more about you."

"You might not like what you find out."

She lifted her chin. "Try me."

She sensed his continued resistance, but then his
shoulders sagged and the fight seeped out of him. "I
don't know where my father is but my guess would
be jail. He was a petty thief who deserted my mother
and me when I was five."

His voice was hard and flat, but she saw hurt in
his eyes. When, she wondered, had she started to be
able to read him?

He dug into the trash bag, pulled out a yellowed
newspaper clipping and handed it to her. The newspaper story wasn't long, probably no more than nine
column inches. The word "embezzled" jumped out
from the headline.

"That's about my mother. She dipped into the
cash register at the beauty shop where she worked
whenever she needed money. It went on for two or
three years before the owner figured it out. She went
to jail when I was nine." He took a deep, rattling
breath. Her chest hurt. "I moved in with my grandparents because I had nowhere else to go. End of
story."

She placed her hand on his arm and felt tension
knotting his muscles. "It wasn't the end of the story.
It was the beginning."

"You're right. I left out the part about my mother not wanting me back when she got out of jail. She checks in once every two or three years, usually to ask for money."

Sara's throat grew so thick she couldn't swallow. "I meant it was the beginning of *your* story."

"You could put it that way. My grandparents made it clear I had plenty to atone for."

"I don't understand. What did *you* have to atone for?"

"I would think that's obvious."

The meaning dawned on her along with growing horror. "You mean because of the wrongs your parents committed? Is that why you went into law enforcement? To balance the scales?"

His shoulders moved up and down in a noncommittal shrug but the answer couldn't have been more clear, especially because she knew him as a man who always tried to do the right thing.

"But how could your grandparents let you take on that burden? You said they were good people."

"They were." Max immediately jumped to their defense. "You can't blame them for making sure I didn't make the same mistakes as my parents."

"But you didn't do anything wrong," she said with heat.

"That doesn't matter. Their blood runs through mine."

"And you think that makes you indebted?" She didn't wait for him to answer. "Well, I think that's ridiculous. A son shouldn't have to pay for the sins of his parents. What your father and mother did has nothing to do with you. You're a good man."

"I am?"

"You always take the moral high ground, even when another route is easier." She took his right hand in both of hers. "Not only that, you're smart and kind and loyal."

She locked gazes with him, hoping he'd recognize her sincerity. A slow smile spread across his face, erasing all traces of the burden that had been so heavy for him to bear. It made him appear years younger.

"Go on," he said lightly. "Tell me what else you like about me."

She pulled her hands free but doubted she succeeded in looking cross. She liked this less serious, playful side of him and wished he'd show it more often. "I already told you."

His eyebrows danced. "You didn't tell me if you thought I was sexy."

"You know I do."

Just like that, the playfulness disappeared and the intimacy they'd shared the night before came rushing back.

"How would I know that?" His smile disappeared, his voice sounding thick.

"Because you're perceptive," she whispered.

He trailed his fingertips down her cheek and across her mouth, letting them linger on her lips. The room had smelled musty when she'd stepped into it, but his intoxicating scent overrode it.

"What if I told you that what I perceive right now is that you want to kiss me?"

His hand moved from her lips and over her cheek to the nape of her neck, where his fingers absently played with her hair. He didn't exert any pressure, didn't try to draw her mouth to his, and she remembered that he was leaving this up to her.

Whether she wanted to make love to him or not was entirely her call.

Her pulse raced with the realization that this was one of those crossroads in life that changed destinies. Choose the safe path, and her life would go on as it always had. Pick the other, and her entire world would change. The moment seemed to stretch forever even when logic told her it lasted but seconds.

"I'd tell you I was right about how perceptive you are," she whispered.

His smile lit up the dark brown of his eyes, making them appear lighter, happier. "Then kiss me, Sara."

They were both on their knees beside the desk. She raised her head until her lips connected with his and kissed him gently, reverently, while her whole body flamed to life, her fatigue forgotten.

He held her head in place with gentle fingers while both of her hands cupped his face. Every part of her, down to the fingers that rested lightly against the stubble on his cheek, felt sensitized.

She could feel her blood pulsing at her throat, in her wrists, in her heart. Warmth spread through her on a languorous path, bringing every part of her to life and centering in a low, heated pool.

Yet everything seemed familiar.

Funny how that was. She could barely recall the kisses of men she'd dated for years. But she'd kissed Max only once before, and the experience was etched in her consciousness as though in indelible ink.

He ran one of his hands down the side of her body in a slow, sensuous slide, then brought it up again.

When his hand reached the side of her breast, she turned her body. His hand glided over her breast, and the warmth turned to heat.

The kiss turned hotter, more demanding, more ravenous. His eyes were open, watching her, which she found as much a turn-on as his kiss.

He broke contact with her mouth, bending his head, burying his face in her neck, sending goose bumps the length of her body. "I'm not going to take anything for granted, Sara. But if you want me to stop, tell me now."

"No," she whispered. His head jerked up. The disappointment that stole over his features didn't have a chance to set in before she clarified, "No, I don't want you to stop."

Max smiled, a flash of white teeth against the Mediterranean cast of his skin.

Untwining her arms from around his neck, he got to his feet, never taking his eyes from hers. She immediately missed the warmth of his body, the stroke of his hands. But then he held out his hand.

"My bedroom's next door," he said.

She gave him her hand, warm flesh against warm flesh, and he helped her to her feet. Hand in hand, they walked to a small masculine bedroom that Sara realized had been his room when he was that lonely boy growing up miles from parents who hadn't cared enough.

A tartan-plaid bedspread covered the double bed, the oak furniture was spartan and he'd already stripped the room of personal belongings aside from a wall clock that ticked away the seconds. Nothing in the room told of the boy he'd been or the man he'd become.

But she knew who he was, and she liked who he

was. She hadn't been exaggerating. She didn't know a better man.

With their hands still linked, he turned toward her and touched her cheek. "Ah, Sara. I can hardly believe you're finally in my bedroom."

"Finally?" Her heart raced, and she imagined she still felt the imprint of his body where it had pressed against hers. "It was only days ago when I asked for your help."

"But I've been imagining this since the first time I saw you." His hand trailed from her cheek to her neck and traced her collarbone. "Even in Texas, there you'd be, in one of my daydreams."

His breathing was slightly uneven, hinting that he might not be as fully in control as he seemed, but he didn't rush to undress her. He was a man who took his time, not a boy who thought there was never enough.

He'd make love that way, too. Slowly, thoroughly. The thought caused sensual shivers to cascade down her body.

She unbelted the nubby yellow robe, and his hands settled on her shoulders, pushing the garment aside so it fell to the floor. She wore her prettiest nightgown, a short, silky shift in a creamy beige with lace at the neckline. Had she worn it because she'd known when she'd packed that she wanted this to happen? Probably, she conceded.

She raised her hands overhead, and his fingertips brushed her hips as he lifted the nightgown. Then her too-large breasts were free, sagging slightly under their own weight. She didn't look at him, not wanting to know if he were disappointed that she wasn't firmer.

"They're perfect." His voice sounded almost worshipful, and she looked into dark eyes hazy with desire. "You're perfect."

Her legs trembled when he hooked his thumbs under the elastic of her panties. She had to anchor a hand on his shoulder as he helped her out of them, the warmth of his palms sliding over her smooth skin.

When she was naked, his gaze roamed over her with as much heat as a summer day in the tropics.

"I always knew you'd be beautiful," he said in a low voice that made her think of sex. "I was right."

She flushed with pleasure while her body trembled with anticipation. It took all her willpower not to jump him and strip off his clothes. "Your turn," she said.

He made quicker work of his clothes, tugging his T-shirt over his head to reveal a hard-muscled, contoured chest sprinkled with a nice amount of dark hair. He pulled his sweatpants and underwear off in one motion.

His legs were long and muscular, as chiseled as his chest. Just when she thought she couldn't stand not touching him any longer, he gathered her to him, skin to bare skin. The room felt hot although she could hear the whirring of the air conditioner. She was hyper aware of her body, from the arch of her foot that rubbed against his to the nipple that he rolled between his thumb and forefinger.

She thought she could even feel the hairs on her arms, which stood at attention.

"Finally," he breathed against her mouth, his voice husky with passion. And then he kissed her, languorously, deeply, as though they had all the time in the world.

They seemed to be moving, but she was so lost in his kiss that she lost track of where they were in the room. But then he sat on the bed, taking her with him so they both fell backward onto the mattress.

He kissed her again and again, deeply, doing delicious things with his lips and tongue that caused lust to tug inside her. The friction of their bodies rubbing against each other drove Sara wild, but Max seemed content to take his time.

His hands, slightly callused from yard work, stroked the dip of her back, the lines of her arms and the curve of her hips until she nearly cried out in frustration.

His large, warm hand closed over her bottom, bringing her more firmly against his erection but not giving her a chance to open her legs to him. His mouth closed over one of her breasts, and desire exploded inside her.

"Going…too…slow," she breathed, her words so choppy and husky she hardly recognized her voice. "Driving…me…crazy."

"That's the idea," he said and put his tongue in her mouth.

She moaned and arrived at the end of her patience. Reaching between their bodies, she found him and closed her hand over his hard shaft. She reveled in his resulting, very male groan.

"You don't play fair." Although his breathing was uneven, his voice wasn't nearly as husky as hers.

She ran her hand up and down his penis. "Not.. playing."

His breathing grew more labored and he stretched one long arm behind him, somehow opening a dresser drawer and withdrawing a condom as she stroked him. Excitement raced through her as he sheathed himself.

His hands glided over her, stopping to gently squeeze her breasts before dipping to her waist and finally reaching the thatch of hair between her thighs.

"I want you, Sara," he said, staring into her eyes as he dipped a finger inside her wet heat. She cried out, then turned and rose up on her knees so she was positioned above him rather than side by side.

Not able to wait a second longer, she lined up her core with his erect penis, settled herself on the head, then lowered her body. She took him inside her, just the first inch.

It was his turn to groan, but he didn't thrust himself off the bed. Slowly, watching his eyes, she lowered herself another inch and then slid herself up his shaft. She repeated the motion, each time taking him another inch deeper before raising on her knees so that he barely penetrated her.

How long, she wondered, could she keep this up?

She lowered herself again, was about to withdraw again when her self-control broke. She settled herself so he filled her to the hilt. In an instant, he'd reversed their positions so that he was on top.

He started to move, finally thrusting into her the way she wanted him to. She gasped at the pleasure, wrapping her legs around his waist. She had her eyes closed, but colors burst behind her eyelids.

When she opened her eyes, she saw him staring down at her. The passion built, the sensation of him watching her intensifying the spiraling pleasure.

She sensed that he held himself back, assuring that she got her release before he took his. But she didn't want to let go. Not yet. She hungered for this incredible feeling to last, to go on and on, but he moved faster.

Unable to help herself, she matched him thrust for thrust as the sensations coiled to a crescendo.

"Max." She clutched at his back as her inner muscles contracted around him and her world came apart. The last thing she saw before her eyes went blind was herself reflected in his hot, brown gaze.

She felt his climax rock through her a moment later, heard his guttural cry, felt his release.

They lay on the bed still joined together for long minutes afterward while their heartbeats slowed and their breaths became more regular. Sara almost cried aloud when he withdrew from her. He got rid of the condom quickly before rejoining her on the bed.

She curled up against him, and he slung an arm over her waist. "Sara," he whispered her name against her hair.

"Hmmm?" she asked.

But she never heard what he said because fatigue finally overtook her and she fell into an exhausted, satisfied sleep.

AN INVISIBLE SOMETHING had been pressing down on Max's heart for so long that he almost failed to recognize the light, airy feeling that replaced it.

Happiness.

"I don't think I've ever seen you do that," Sara remarked.

They'd stopped at a traffic light in the heart of Baltimore, a few miles from the Johns Hopkins nursing school where she had a class that started in ten minutes.

He knew she usually preferred to arrive much earlier, but they'd made love again that morning, with him taking pains to go even slower than before.

She looked demure in her nursing school uniform, which consisted of a short-sleeved white polo shirt worn with navy-blue pants, white socks and shoes. Last night and this morning, she'd been anything but demure. The happiness hit him again. "You've never seen me do what?"

"Smile when you're in FBI-guy mode."

He felt his smile grow wider. But, damn it. He couldn't help it. "What's FBI-guy mode?"

"Dark sunglasses, crisp clothing, firm chin, determined expression, touch-me-not attitude."

The light turned green, and he maneuvered the car with the flow of traffic. He caught another red light in the next block and slid her a suggestive look. "Honey, you can touch me any time you like."

Her mouth curved. "Do you really mean that?"

"I really mean that."

"Okay." Her hand covered his, which rested on the gear shift between their seats. By the time he'd figured out she intended to put the car in park, she'd taken off his sunglasses and placed them on the dash. Then she cupped the back of his head and pulled his mouth down to hers.

Max's inclination was to pull back and tell her kissing in public wasn't a good idea, but then she slipped her tongue between his lips. He moaned and sank into a kiss so hot it seared his insides. He let himself go, the way he hadn't last night or this morning.

He'd wanted her so badly that sweat had beaded his brow but he'd forced himself to go slow. The leisurely pace had almost killed him, but he couldn't let on that he wanted her with the desperation of a wild beast.

The desperation was back. He longed to drive into her right here and now, but the blaring car horns behind them saved him from revealing his baser instinct. He reluctantly broke off the kiss.

"We're lucky we didn't get pulled over." He replaced his sunglasses, put the car in drive and rejoined reality, surprised that he wasn't ashamed for indulging in public.

She smiled, flipping down the car's sun visor and using the mirror to refasten her hair. "Couples don't get pulled over for necking at red lights."

"Yes, they do. I've pulled over a few myself." He slanted her a wry look. "Although the couples in question were usually in their teens."

"Don't tell me you wrote them tickets!"

He'd threatened as much, but didn't think she'd be receptive to hearing that. "Mostly I warned them to pay attention to the road."

From the corner of his eye, he saw her wince. Her skin was becomingly flushed and her lips swollen from his kisses, and he suddenly understood something he hadn't when he'd turned on the patrol car's flashing lights and frightened those teenagers.

"If I were still a cop, I wouldn't pull them over. I'd blow my horn and let them go."

From her smile, he could tell his comment pleased her. "Really? What's changed?"

He'd fallen in love. The knowledge hit him hard and fast, the same way it had after they'd made love the night before. But this was the wrong place and wrong time to tell Sara he loved her. It had been the wrong time last night, too, but she'd drifted to sleep before she'd heard him.

"I learned you have to take your happiness where you can get it," he said. "Even if it's at a red light."

But it was more than that. It was even more than the realization that he loved Sara. Max now understood that some things were more important than the letter of the law. Sara was more important.

At the curb in front of the nursing school, he put the car in park. This time he was the one who initiated another dizzying kiss. When they finally tore their mouths apart, she gazed at him with huge eyes. "If you asked me to skip class, I would. We could be at my place in minutes."

He wanted to accept her offer so badly he ached, but again he warned himself to slow down. "I'd like nothing better, but we both have things to do."

Her lower lip quivered, but then she smiled, nodded and opened the car door. He watched her until she was inside the building, then leaned back against his headrest and came to terms with the truth.

He loved Sara.

He loved her because she was good and kind and loyal and caring. But he also loved her because with some well-chosen words and a little faith, she'd helped him realize he was a good man.

She was right. His parents' mistakes had been theirs alone, and he couldn't keep paying for them. He'd continue to try to do the right thing, but it was time he acknowledged things were neither as black nor as white as he'd always believed.

He'd always done things the hard way, following the letter of the law as he investigated crimes, never once circumventing the rules. But if bending the occasional rule would achieve the greater good, he needed to give himself permission to bend it.

Keeping the woman he loved out of harm's way qualified, but the only way to do that was to find Larry. And he was fresh out of leads.

He ducked into the first parking lot he spotted, found an empty corner and put his car in neutral. Taking his cell phone from the clip on his belt, he dialed information and had the computer connect him to the local phone company. "Honey Williams, please."

She came on the line within minutes, saying that she sure did remember him and acknowledging she was still dating a city cop. He answered her questions about how the FBI was treating him, then got to the point.

Because Honey Williams was somebody cops went to when they needed to bend the rules.

"I wouldn't ask if it wasn't important, Honey, but I need the phone records of a guy named Larry Brunell."

"TELL ME AGAIN why you aren't going in to work tonight." Max took a red winter dress earmarked for a large cardboard box from a hanger in his grandmother's bedroom closet and paused in the act of folding it.

"Because I called in sick," Sara said.

At his look of dismay, she stood on tiptoes and kissed him on the lips. "I'm kidding, Mr. Do the Right Thing. They do give me a night off every once in a while, you know."

"Yeah, but you could have taken it to do something more enjoyable than helping me pack up my grandparents' things," he said as he finished folding the dress and bent to pack it into the box.

She put her hands on her hips, surprised he felt that way. "Helping you is the least I can do after all you've done for me."

He straightened, shaking his head as he did so. "I haven't done anything yet."

"Are you kidding? You're keeping me safe."

He shrugged. "I'm not positive you're in danger. The guy who broke into your house could have been a common burglar. And let's not forget, I haven't found Larry yet."

"You *will* find him." Her voice held conviction. "Didn't you say you were expecting some information tomorrow that could provide a new lead?"

He nodded.

She smiled determinedly, trying not to dwell on the fact that time was growing short. It was already Tuesday night. Ralph was due to come looking for his money at noon Friday.

"Then let's try to forget about Larry and Johnny for tonight and concentrate on you." She surveyed the room, but her gaze snagged on Max's T-shirt. It depicted a comical drawing of a terrapin, which was the University of Maryland's mascot, and the saying, Fear the Turtle.

"Cute," she said.

He glanced down at his chest, then back up at her. "Do you mean me or the T-shirt?"

She laughed, then really looked at him. The silly T-shirt hugged the muscular planes of his chest but left his muscular arms bare. His legs were bare, too, under a pair of shorts she wished were shorter. Her mouth went dry.

"Cute isn't the word I'd use to describe you," she said. "You need a much more potent word like... sizzling."

He laughed, although she'd been serious.

"Okay," he said. "What do you want to do first?"

You, she thought.

"You tell me," she said, hoping he'd pick up on the suggestion in her voice and the heat in her eyes.

"How about packing up whatever's in the dresser drawers in the guest bedroom? There's not much in there, so it'll make it feel like we're making good progress."

Swallowing her disappointment, she nodded and went to work. She told herself not to read too much into what had just happened. Although she doubted he could have missed the fact that she'd wanted to make love to him then and there, that wasn't why she was here. She was here to work, and there was plenty of work to go around.

They spent the better part of three hours tackling dressers and closets in the second-floor bedrooms before moving downstairs to the coat closet.

A boy's ski jacket they found in the back of the closet was the last to go into the box. Sara helped Max wrestle with the flaps at the top of the box until they'd managed to close it, then sat down on top of it.

"There," she said. "All done."

He stood back, smiling at her. The smile was innocent, but still lust licked at her insides, the way it had every time she'd looked at him tonight.

"I don't know about that," he said. "There's another desk in the living room that we could go through."

She anchored her hands on either side of her and pushed up from the box, then walked deliberately to where he stood and linked her hands around the back of his neck.

"Not tonight," she said. "Tonight I can think of a better way to spend our time."

"Oh, yeah," he said, the smile growing wider as she inched her mouth nearer to his. He smelled of chocolate, and she figured he must have a stash somewhere in the house she didn't know about. "And what would that be?"

"This," she said and kissed him. The lust she'd been trying to suppress all night exploded, spiraling inside her like a whirlwind.

He kissed her back with a mastery that dizzied her, dipping again and again into the well of her mouth until she felt as though she'd been drugged.

She pressed against him, feeling desire pool and throb. If she hadn't been hanging on to the turtle on the front of his T-shirt, she wasn't sure her legs could have supported her.

"I've got to give it to you. You can really kiss." She meant to sound teasing, but instead her voice shook.

He lowered his head and put his mouth near her ear. Shivers ran down her body at the feel of his soft breath against her skin. "There are some other things I do particularly well. If you come to the bedroom, I'll show you."

She trailed three fingers down his chest, then boldly feathered them over his erection. "What if I don't want to wait?"

His eyes glowed and for a moment she thought he would jam her up against the wall and tear off her clothes so he could bury himself in her. As though he needed to make love to her, the way she needed him inside her.

A muscle in his jaw worked but he restrained himself. His hands were on her body, but they weren't frantic. He seemed to enjoy touching her, but didn't act as though he couldn't help but touch her.

"Good things come to those who wait," he quipped, then carefully swept her up in his arms.

He carried her up the stairs, as though he were Rhett Butler and she Scarlet O'Hara. It should have been one of the most romantic moments of her life, a memory that would always have the power to make her swoon.

But foremost in her mind was that she'd been carried away by the moment, willing and eager to do him in the hallway, while he'd managed to restrain himself with heartbreaking ease. The same way he'd restrained himself earlier that night.

Somewhere along the way she'd allowed herself to need him, but needing him was no healthier than getting hooked on a drug. Because he didn't need her back. Not physically. Not emotionally.

Instead of setting her down when they reached the mouth of his bedroom, he stepped sideways so he could carry her across the threshold.

She tried to close her mind to images of a flowing white dress, clinking champagne glasses and happily ever after. She couldn't afford to think that way, not when he could be gone from her life by the end of the week.

Before she could build her defenses, he lowered his head and captured her mouth in a kiss as sweet as it was hot. Again, there was nothing urgent about his kiss. Again, her nerve endings went haywire.

Logically she knew he stood still as he kissed her, but her world spun anyway, because she could no longer escape the truth.

She'd gone and foolishly fallen in love with Max Dolinger.

9

HEDGE CLIPPER IN HAND, Max stood back and surveyed the newly trimmed azalea bushes in the front yard as the sun rose fractionally higher in the sky. He estimated it wasn't yet eight o'clock.

He'd awakened at about six-thirty with Sara's naked body curled against his, her hand resting trustingly over his heart as she slept. He'd gotten an erection before his eyes had fully opened.

It would have been easy to awaken her with a kiss, easier still to slip inside her and start the morning the same delightful way they'd ended the night.

Instead he'd ignored his body's urgent message and quietly slipped out of bed. He'd pulled some old clothes from a dresser drawer, stealthily left the room and tackled the bushes at sunrise.

He'd sheared off the excess growth and packed it into a yard bag, all the while fighting an overwhelming desire to rush back up the stairs.

The damnable thing was that Sara would welcome him back into bed, but fast and furious wasn't his style. Now that Sara had let him into her bed, he'd get her slowly accustomed to his presence.

After a time, maybe she'd let him into her heart as well.

He dragged the single yard bag to the curb, where a truck would pick it up later that afternoon. Then he splashed water from the outside spigot onto his face and hands before walking into the house.

He heard a cupboard door open, followed quickly by a clatter of pans and a loud oath. "Stupid pans."

Again it struck him that the house, which had seemed almost unbearably empty with his grandparents gone, had life. He grinned and stopped at the mouth to the kitchen, where he had a view of Sara picking up pots and pans from the floor.

She'd slept in nothing but her skin last night but now wore an old T-shirt of his that left most of her legs exposed. She looked unbearably sexy.

"Who shoved those pans in the cupboard like that anyway?" she muttered to herself.

"That would be my grandmother. She could organize a kick-ass fundraiser but never could get it together in the kitchen."

The frying pan in Sara's hand dropped to the floor with another clank, and her head jerked toward him.

"Good morning." He let his smile break free and waited for her expression to soften, the way it had last night.

"Morning," she replied, avoiding his gaze. She bent to pick up the pot and shoved it into the cupboard no less haphazardly than his grandmother used to. "I can't seem to find the coffeemaker."

He nodded to the one on the counter half-hidden by an ancient toaster oven and watched her move it to an empty spot. "The coffee's in that skinny drawer beside the sink."

She murmured a thank you but still didn't look at him as she retrieved the coffee and dumped it into the coffeemaker.

She didn't ask for an explanation about where he'd been, but he gave one anyway. "I was pruning the bushes in the front yard. I tried my best not to wake you."

"You didn't. But I had to get up anyway. It's Wednesday, right? I have a class at ten."

He frowned at her tone. While not cool, it was far from warm. "Something wrong?"

Her eyes darted to his, then away. "No. Nothing's wrong. It's just that I'm not a morning person."

"Maybe I can turn you into one."

He moved across the room, took her face in his hands and kissed her. Now that he knew how she liked to be kissed, he took full advantage, teasing and tasting until her lips softened. Then he slanted his mouth over hers and plundered.

He slid his hand under her shirt. His disappointment at finding panties vanished when his hand ventured higher and discovered her bare breast. He filled his palm with the soft flesh and let his fingers go to work on her nipple.

"That making me into a morning person…" Her voice held a delightful shake. "…That's just an excuse so you can have your way with me."

"Do I need an excuse?" he asked, but it was a rhetorical question and he didn't expect an answer.

His head descended, but she stopped his mouth from covering hers by pressing two fingers against his lips. He kissed her fingertips.

Her eyes looked uncertain when they raised to

his, but then he ran a thumb over her already taut nipple. She sighed and he sensed her capitulation.

"No, you don't need an excuse," she said, her voice breathy. And this time, she kissed him.

SARA STRIPPED OFF HER CLOTHES and stood in front of the bedroom closet in her row house, pulling out a navy-blue skirt and a white short-sleeved shirt.

When she realized she'd forgotten her other nursing school uniform, she'd asked Max to stop by her place on the way to class this morning. He waited for her downstairs, probably sneaking cookies out of the cookie jar.

Her heart swelled at the thought of him, her body still tingling with the afterglow of their morning lovemaking.

But her brain knew she was a fool. A great, big, stupid fool who should have known better than to get involved with a man like Max.

She knew his history. She knew he was basically a loner who didn't need anybody but himself. And she knew he was going back to Texas soon.

Friday night, to be exact. She'd seen his return plane ticket on the kitchen table this morning before he'd come into the house from pruning the bushes. Why hadn't she considered that he was leaving soon and possibly never coming back when she'd decided to sleep with him?

The fears had crept in last night when she'd been out of her mind with wanting him and he'd been so in control. When she'd thought about it, she'd realized he'd had that cool control every time they made love.

She'd begun to need him, but he only wanted her. Because Max Dolinger didn't need anybody.

And still she'd gone and fallen for him.

What's worse, she didn't seem to have any will-power where he was concerned. She'd halfway convinced herself to tell him this morning that they should slow things down, yet her resolve had faded to nothing when he'd touched her.

"Sara, time's getting short," Max yelled up the stairs. "If we don't leave soon, you'll be late for class."

It dawned on her that she was standing at the closet, clothes in hand, making no move to get dressed.

"Just a few more minutes," she called back.

Pulling herself together, she dressed quickly, then shut off her bedroom light. She ducked into the bathroom, checking herself in the mirror to make sure her hair was in place and her makeup on straight.

She expected misery to cloud her face but instead her skin glowed and her eyes shone. Her lips, still slightly swollen from Max's kisses, were rosy even without lipstick. She looked like a woman who had been well and truly loved.

She blinked back tears.

Refusing to feel sorry for herself, she turned from the mirror. Max had left the decision to get involved entirely up to her. He hadn't made any guarantees. Not only hadn't he promised her forever, he hadn't promised her next week.

She'd known all along that he was selling his grandparents' house, effectively cutting ties with the area. She should have thought about what the ramifications would be to her.

She reached the top of the stairs and squared her shoulders, preparing to act as if nothing were bothering her.

A faint chirping that seemed to be coming from Johnny's bedroom stopped her.

Puzzled, she went into his room to investigate. The room was as he'd left it, the bed unmade, clothes scattered here and there on the floor, a pile of paper on his desk.

The chirping continued.

She switched on the light. Following the sound, she ventured deeper into the room. The sound seemed to be coming from his desk drawer. Opening it, she found the culprit—one of those thick black digital wristwatches with a built-in alarm.

She picked it up, clicked the off button and was about to drop the watch back into the desk drawer when a name on a piece of paper caught her eye.

Ralph Abernathy.

The breath snagged in her throat. Ralph was the first name of the man who'd bought the baseball with the fake autograph, the man Johnny said he had no idea how to contact.

Yet scrawled below the name was a telephone number.

"Sara, are you coming?"

Max's voice again, urging her to hurry. She put the watch back in the drawer, then hesitated before snatching up the piece of paper.

Her first inclination was to show Max what she'd found so they could figure out what it meant together, but her mind raced ahead to what would happen if she did.

The obvious conclusion was that Johnny had lied when he'd claimed not to know how to contact the buyer. Why should she prejudice Max against her brother if that weren't the case?

What if the name on the paper belonged to some other Ralph? She should at least give Johnny a chance to explain before damning him in the eyes of a man whose help he was depending on.

Making up her mind, she stuffed the piece of paper into her skirt pocket and went downstairs.

MAX PULLED TO THE CURB in front of the nursing school five minutes before Sara's class was due to begin and only ten minutes before Honey Williams had arranged to meet him at a local CVS with a printout of Larry's phone records.

"I'm supposed to pick you up at five o'clock, right?" he asked before she could slip out of the car.

She looked at him blankly for a minute before his question seemed to register. "Five o'clock. Yeah, that's right."

He frowned at her. She'd been preoccupied all morning, but more so since they'd stopped at her house. "Is everything all right, Sara?"

"Everything's fine. It's just that I'm running late." She opened the car door, swung one leg out, then turned back. "You're not still concerned about me leaving the building during the day, are you? I mean, you don't think the guy looking for Larry would try anything in broad daylight?"

"No, but I would still rather you not be alone," Max said slowly. "Why? What's this about?"

"I have a break today at one-thirty," she said. "I'm thinking about calling Johnny and asking him to meet me for a late lunch."

"Why not eat at the school cafeteria?"

She shook her head. "We did that once, and Johnny felt uncomfortable. But there's a restaurant a block from here called the Dugout that he likes."

"Then ask him to meet you at the security desk so you can go there together," Max suggested. He didn't have a problem with Sara walking a block in broad daylight if Johnny were with her.

"Good idea," she said.

"Thanks for telling me."

An indentation appeared between her brows and something he couldn't identify flashed in her eyes. "I better run."

Before she could slip out of the car, he caught her wrist. "You're forgetting something."

He heard her suck in a breath and she looked vaguely panicked. "What?"

"This," he said and kissed her soundly on the mouth. Her lips clung reassuringly to his for a moment, and the familiar heat came flooding back.

Before she got out of the car, she touched his cheek, looking contented and wistful at once. Then she was gone.

Her odd behavior nagged at Max, but he didn't have time to puzzle over it because fifteen minutes later he was sitting in the parking lot outside the CVS looking over Larry's phone records.

Honey had handed over the printout minutes ago, murmuring an apology for not being able to get him the information the day before. Then she'd slipped out of the drugstore like she was on a covert mission.

As Max finished the last of the Hershey's bars he'd bought while waiting in CVS, he surveyed the list of numbers, hoping one would jump out at him.

Larry hadn't made any recent calls from his cell phone, but a couple dozen calls originated from his land line. The printout contained numbers only, but it would be easy enough to use a computer at a public library to cross-check numbers with names and addresses.

A better idea occurred to him. Max dug into his pocket and unfolded the list Sara had given him, on which he'd written down phone numbers. As he suspected, quite a few of the numbers belonged to Larry's friends and relatives. He got busy dialing the ones that didn't.

He got the Rusty Nail Pub on the first try and an answering machine for a sporting-goods store on the second, but struck gold on the third.

"The Ten Count," a gravelly female voice answered.

He recognized the name of the gym immediately. The suspicious guy at the bar claimed to own the place.

His pulse sped up, but he strived to make his voice sound normal when he asked for directions. Then he hung up and considered what this newest development meant.

The owner of the gym didn't fit the description of the man who'd broken into Sara's house, but he felt damn sure Larry's call to the gym hadn't been a coincidence. He put his car in gear.

The Ten Count was located on the outskirts of the city in a bank of low-sitting warehouses. The second building to the right, between a catering company and a furniture warehouse.

Max parked in one of a few dozen empty spaces, then quickly climbed the three concrete steps and let himself inside. The interior of the place was unremarkable, with a boxing ring located in the rear and other sections partitioned off for weight training and sparring.

It had neither a reception desk nor a lobby, and the only signs of life were a short, bald man pummeling a punching bag and another man skipping rope. A sign on the wall said, Punch First, Ask Questions Later.

Somebody sneezed, and Max noticed a tiny office tucked in the front corner of the building. An elderly, gray-haired woman was inside the office, sitting behind a desk and dabbing at her nose.

She peered at him above wire-rimmed reading glasses when he stopped at the threshold of the open door. "What you need?"

The same voice from the telephone.

"I'm thinking about taking up boxing," Max ad-libbed. "Can you tell me about this place?"

She gave him the once-over. "Be a shame to mess up that face of yours, but this here's what you call a recreational gym. You can either box for exercise or take it serious."

She continued with a spiel that sounded practiced. He waited until she was through, smiled and went for the personal touch. "Sounds like you're sold on this place. Have you worked here long?"

She smiled back, her teeth so white and regular against her wrinkled skin they had to be dentures. "I help out when I can."

On the wall behind her hung a large photo of a referee raising a shaggy-haired boxer's right arm in victory. Upon closer inspection, Max recognized the boxer as a younger, hairier version of the man from the pub.

"I see you've trained a number of champions," he remarked.

She glanced at the photo, then beamed. "That's my grandson Art Skalecky, though everybody calls him Rocky on account of he looks like Sylvester Stallone."

Max didn't see any resemblance other than dark hair, most of which Skalecky no longer had, but refrained from commenting. "So your grandson Rocky owns this place?"

"He and his brother Brad own it together." She pointed to a photo of another boxer, this one noticeably taller and less beefy. He fit the description of the man who'd broken into Sara's house.

Max searched his mind for a platitude even as it whirled with theories. "You must be proud of them."

"They're good boys. I should know. I raised them myself. Those two, they have hearts of gold. They'd do anything for me."

"Are they here?"

"They get here at two in the afternoon and work till evening. They're like clockwork, those boys." Her posture grew tense, suspicious. "Why?"

"I need to talk to them."

Her eyes narrowed shrewdly. "You're not really interested in boxing, are you?"

"I'm more interested in a friend of mine who's missing." Bringing up the calls Larry had made to the gym would label him law enforcement, which Max sensed would be the wrong move. "He's mentioned the gym so I thought somebody here might know something."

"What's his name?"

"Larry Brunell. He bartends over at the Rusty Nail Pub."

"Brunell? That's the bastard who swindled me!"

Max's heartbeat quickened. "How so?"

The woman's face reddened. "I'm at the park reading my newspaper. Bastard picks up something from the ground, says it's a lottery ticket, asks if it's mine. I say it isn't. It's not his either, so he says it's ours. He says we should check the numbers in the newspaper, that he'll share with me if we win."

"Let me guess. The ticket was a winner?"

"Not the big winner, a smaller one. But big enough that it's got to be cashed at lottery headquarters. But headquarters closes at four-thirty and it's nearly that now. He says he's going out of town the next morning. What should we do?"

The scam was a popular one, so Max easily guessed what came next. "He suggested you give him half the winnings, keep the ticket and cash it in without him."

"He got me to suggest it. My bank was around the corner and still open. He said he'd take less than half 'cause I had to go to more trouble."

Max winced, appalled that Larry had sunk so low to take advantage of an old woman. Even if she were greedy. "Was the ticket forged?"

For the first time the woman looked sheepish. "It was real enough, but it was for the wrong day. I got so excited when the numbers matched it didn't sink in that the newspaper listed yesterday's winners and the ticket was from that day."

"Did you go to the police?"

She scowled. "Wouldn't trust a copper farther than I could throw him, not after my Brad ended up in jail for something he didn't do. I did something better. I told my grandsons."

The wheels in Max's head spun hard. Larry had played the odds by choosing an elderly victim, but he'd erred badly by picking one with scary family connections.

"Bastard underestimated me. Didn't tell him he looked familiar. My cousin has a dry cleaners on O'Donnell Square and I remembered him going into that pub. Rusty's. Turned out he works there."

"So you sent your grandsons after him?"

She nodded. "Would you believe the bastard calls me here at the gym asking me to call off my boys? Says he needs more time to get the money together. I told him to go to hell."

Larry hadn't gone to hell, but he had gotten out of town. He'd left behind not one, but two angry victims—and an accomplice who'd helped him on at least one of the jobs.

"Thanks for the information," Max said and left the office.

He'd barely gotten past the door frame when she yelled after him, "If you find this Brunell, I want a piece of him."

Max acknowledged her with a short wave, identifying with the sentiment. But right now, the man Max wanted a piece of was Johnny Reynolds. And he knew where to find him.

The Dugout, having lunch with his sister.

THE SCENT OF BURGERS frying on the grill and pizza baking in the restaurant's brick oven filled the Dugout, but Sara's stomach churned with nervousness instead of hunger.

Johnny sat across from her in a wooden booth near the back of a restaurant that was still bustling even though the lunch-hour rush was largely over. As he looked over the choices with his head bent over a menu, he chewed his bottom lip, a habit he'd developed in childhood.

A wave of love hit her. She'd babysat for him so often in her teenage years that it had begun to feel as though he were as much her child as their parents'.

She hardened herself before the love made her weak and concentrated on a much uglier reality. Johnny had lied.

A case could be made that she'd lied, too. By omission in not immediately alerting Max of her suspicion that Johnny knew how to contact the buyer of the baseball.

She'd rationalized that she needed to hear her brother's explanation first, but knew in her heart she feared what Max would do if he decided Johnny had deliberately passed off a fake autograph.

"How's the search going?" Johnny asked after they ordered. A cheeseburger for him, a chicken Caesar salad for her.

"Max has a couple leads he's chasing down, but it could be going better. Larry seems to have dropped off the face of the earth."

Johnny nodded, then picked up his glass and gulped Coke with the gusto of a young boy. A wave of protectiveness washed over her. There had to be a good reason for his lie. There just had to be.

He peered at her over his glass with eyes that reminded her of the ones she saw in the mirror every day. "Something on your mind? You seem jumpy."

She wordlessly pulled the piece of scrap paper out of her pocket. Noticing that her hands trembled when she unfolded it, she set it in front of him. She knew her brother well enough to pick up on the tension that settled over him as he stared down at Ralph Abernathy's name and phone number.

"Where did you get this?" Johnny asked without looking up.

"When we stopped at the house today, an alarm in your room went off. I went to investigate and found a digital watch in your desk drawer. I also found this."

"Did you show it to Mr. Dolinger?" he asked, and her slim hope faded that Ralph Abernathy wasn't the same Ralph who'd bought the baseball.

"No, I didn't show it to Max. I wanted to ask you about it first." She covered her stomach with her right hand, but the action did nothing to soothe her nausea. "What's going on, Johnny?"

When Johnny's eyes finally met hers, they were beseeching. "It's not how it looks."

"Then you didn't lie about not knowing how to contact the man who bought the baseball?"

He fidgeted in his chair and his eyes slid away from her. "I can explain."

"He needs to explain to me, too."

Sara jerked her head up to see a grim-faced Max staring down at them. Of course. She'd told him where she and Johnny were having lunch.

Her breath caught. She loved Max, but she wasn't glad to see him. Her fears of what he'd do if her brother proved to be guilty surfaced, and her palms grew damp. Because, oh Lord, she feared Johnny might be just that.

Max slid into the booth next to her without being asked, forcing Sara to move over. Then he picked up the piece of paper containing Ralph's name and phone number.

Max turned his head to stare at her, but not with that impassive expression she couldn't read. He looked pained. "You found this at your place this morning. That's why you were preoccupied in the car."

She closed her eyes briefly, feeling that pain as if it were her own. By the time she opened them, a mask had come over his face.

"I can explain why I didn't tell you," she said, her guilt at having hurt him warring with her protective instincts for her brother. "Johnny—"

"Save it, Sara. I know your brother's involved in the cons Larry is running." His unfriendly gaze slanted to Johnny. "Aren't you, Johnny?"

Her brother chewed on his lower lip in that way he had when he was mulling over something. Sara feared it might be his options. "Why would you say that?"

"I tracked down an old lady who knew Larry. Turned out he conned her into giving him money for a winning lottery ticket that didn't turn out to be a winner."

A hand felt as though it were squeezing Sara's throat, making it difficult for her to breathe.

"I don't know anything about that, man." Johnny raised his hands palms out. "If Larry did that, he did it on his own."

Max's expression hardened. "Larry didn't con Ralph Abernathy on his own. You were in on it with him."

Sara stared at her brother, willing him to deny

Max's accusation but already knowing that he wouldn't. Johnny ran a hand over his lower face and it seemed an eternity before he answered. He looked far older than his eighteen years.

"Yes," he said gravely. "I was in on the con with him."

10

MAX COULD HAVE KICKED himself. Hard. He should have been more suspicious of Johnny from the outset. And he would have been if not for Sara. Sara, who'd obviously figured out what was going on and tried to hide it from him. Damn, he was a fool.

"Larry and I both knew the autograph was fake from the beginning." Johnny stared down at his hands, which he'd folded on the table. His voice grew quiet, and Max had to listen carefully to hear him above the clinking of silverware and murmur of voices. "Larry came up with the plan, but I went along with it. I'd been trying to fool people with that baseball for so long, I never thought the old guy would go for it."

"Johnny, how could you?" Sara asked in a voice no louder than a whisper, but Max was careful not to look at her. He didn't want to be swayed by the hurt he felt sure would be etched on her face.

Johnny looked miserable when he focused on his sister. "I'm sorry, Sara. I admit it. I screwed up."

"Just tell us what really happened," Max said.

Johnny took a deep breath, then squared his shoulders. He seemed to gather strength from deep inside himself. "After I showed Larry the autograph, he told me about this movie he'd seen about con men. He told me how easy it looked. He said he thought we could fool somebody into thinking the autograph was genuine.

"He found the old guy, Ralph Abernathy, at a baseball-card show at the mall. He told him about the ball and set up a meet, but not at the Blue Plate Diner. We met at a Chinese place in Fell's Point."

"You thought we'd figure out you were in on the con if we tracked down Ralph and heard his side of the story?" Max ventured, the very possibility that had occurred to him when he and Sara had visited the diner.

Johnny nodded. "That's right."

"Go on," Max prodded when the kid again lapsed into silence.

"I thought it was a no-risk proposition. If Ralph said the ball was fake, I'd pretend to be surprised. Ralph, he's no dummy. He was excited about the autograph but asked for a certificate of authentication. I didn't even know what that was. But Larry, he pulled out a certificate. Turns out he has a COA— that's what they call it—for Barbarellen, his sculpture. He had a fake one made for the autograph.

"I knew we'd stepped over the line, but I didn't know how to cross back over it. Larry told Ralph somebody else was interested in buying the ball but we'd sell it to him then and there if he gave us a cashier's check."

"And you let him go to his bank and get one?" Sara sounded both incredulous and hurt.

"Sara, could you let your brother finish the story?" Max's voice sounded sharp, but he couldn't help that. He was angry at both brother and sister.

Johnny hesitated only slightly before continuing. "We gave him the ball and split the money, but I had second thoughts almost immediately. I tried calling Larry to tell him I didn't feel right about what we'd done, but I couldn't get him on the phone."

"Before or after Ralph tracked you down?"

"Both, but I don't expect you to believe that," Johnny answered. He was right. Max believed the kid's second thoughts had a direct correlation to the duped buyer showing up and demanding his money back. "I didn't get really worried, though, until Ralph came into the coffee shop. He had the fake ball and the fake COA, which were plenty enough to incriminate me."

"How did he find you?"

Johnny grimaced. "Stupidity on my part. When we met with him, I'd just come from work and my shirt had the Coffee Ground's logo on it. He said it was easy to find me."

Although Sara kept quiet, Max felt disapproval rolling off her in waves. And rightfully so. Larry and Johnny had found the old-timer's weakness, in this case a passion for baseball, and had exploited it. That was a tactic of con men the world round.

Johnny lapsed into silence, so Max finished the story for him. "Ralph wanted his money back or else. You only had half of it and Larry was gone. So you made up a story so Sara would help you find him."

Johnny nodded, looking miserable. He was barely able to meet his sister's eyes. "I'm sorry, Sara. I should have told you the truth."

"Yes, you should have," Sara said tightly.

Max had to fight to keep from rolling his eyes. Talk about the lying pot calling the kettle black.

Johnny leaned across the table, balancing his weight on his forearms. His eyes panned from Sara to Max. "But I'm not lying now. You've got to believe me. I had nothing to do with the old lady and the lottery ticket."

Max crossed his arms over his chest, feeling doubly duped. "Since you're being so honest, in the interest of full disclosure, why don't you tell me about the other trouble you got yourself into."

Brother and sister exchanged a look, but Sara broke first. "You know about Johnny's juvenile record?"

Oxygen temporarily left his lungs, and it was a moment before he could speak. "What juvenile record?"

Her eyes got big. "Isn't that what you were talking about?"

"Juvenile records are sealed. They don't generally show up on background checks. But when you're eighteen or over and you're caught shoplifting, that comes up."

"Shoplifting?" Sara's surprise was so marked, it had to be genuine. Her gaze ricocheted to her brother. "When were you arrested for shoplifting?"

Johnny stared down at the table, seeming to gather his thoughts. Max sat back, curious to see how he'd handle this. He couldn't lie because Max obviously already knew the details, but he could spin the story to his advantage.

"It was about eight months ago, not that long after we moved to Florida. I stopped at a music store with two guys I'd just met. I wanted to impress them, so I shoved two CDs in my pocket and tried to walk out without paying. I got caught."

"But why didn't I know about this?" Sara asked.

"I asked Mom and Dad not to tell you." Johnny sighed heavily. "It was bad enough that they knew. After everything you'd been through with me, Sara, I didn't want you to know, too."

"Did those men you were with dare you to steal the CDs? Is that why you did it?" Sara tried to shift the blame away from her brother, where Max thought it rightfully belonged. Max waited, sure Johnny would take the easy out.

"There's no excuse for what I did, Sara. I shouldn't have done it. Period."

His answer earned Max's grudging respect, but he wasn't ready to label Johnny Reynolds a reformed saint yet. "Tell me about your juvenile record."

Johnny looked him straight in the eye. "Me and some friends stole a car when I was fifteen. We'd all been drinking, and none of us were old enough to drive. We crashed. The other driver went to the hospital with a concussion and a broken leg. We went to juvenile hall."

"But that was it," Sara was quick to add. "It was his first offense and after he got out of juvenile hall, he didn't get into any more trouble."

"Not exactly," Johnny said. "I had trouble adjusting to my new high school when I moved to Florida with my parents so I did something stupid and stopped going to class. That's why I'm working on my GED."

Max admired the put-the-blame-on-me way Johnny spelled out the facts, but he wasn't sold on the kid. Johnny not only had a history of trouble, but he'd already admitted that he'd initially lied about being in on the Ralph Abernathy con.

"Let's get back to Larry and the lottery ticket," Max said. "I'm asking you for the last time, what do you know about it?"

"Nothing," Johnny said. "I'm telling the truth, man. After we got the money from Ralph, I didn't even talk to Larry again."

"So he never mentioned a gym called the Ten Count?"

"No. Why?"

Max didn't see any reason not to answer his question. "Two brothers, Rocky and Brad Skalecky, own the gym. They're ex-boxers. Their grandmother is the woman Larry conned with the lottery ticket. She didn't go to the police for help. She went to her grandsons."

Sara covered her mouth with her right hand, the meaning of his discovery obviously not lost on her. Max finally looked at her and had to fight his impulse to reach out and comfort her.

"Rocky Skalecky has been hanging around the Rusty Nail," he told her. "I think he's waiting to see if Larry will show. I also think your house was broken into because he found out you and Larry used to live together and thought Larry might be hiding out there."

"But it wasn't Rocky Skalecky who broke into my house," Sara said. "I've seen him at the pub, and he's too short to be the same guy."

"Remember what I said about Rocky having a brother? His brother's much taller than he is."

Johnny let out a harsh gasp. "You think Brad Skalecky broke into Sara's place?"

Max nodded. "I'm almost certain of it. The brothers want their grandmother's money back. They're boxers. They're tough guys. They might also want revenge."

The waitress who came to their table carrying plates of food put a temporary halt to their conversation. She handed Max a menu he didn't ask for, told him she'd be back shortly and left.

"I need to go," Johnny announced, rising and winding through the tables toward the exit before Max could protest.

"Wait here," Max told Sara and got to his feet. He caught up with the teenager a few steps outside the door and restrained him with a firm hand on his shoulder. "Don't even think about it."

Johnny's skin was flushed, his chest heaving. "How would you know what I'm thinking?"

"You're thinking about charging into the Ten Count and confronting the guys who have been messing with your sister. If they don't leave her alone, you'll threaten to bust their heads." Max raised his eyebrows. "How am I doing so far?"

Johnny's eyes glittered. "You can't stop me."

"Yes, I can. And so can the Skalecky brothers. Think, Johnny. They're pro boxers. Confronting them would be stupid."

The teenager blew air through his nose. "I have to do something. This is Sara we're talking about."

"You've already done enough," Max said in a low, furious voice. "If you hadn't conned Ralph Abernathy and lied about it, none of this would have happened."

Even though Max was the bigger man, Johnny took a step toward him until they were nose to nose. "Don't you think I know that? I'm sorry, okay?"

"And you think sorry is enough? That it'll make it all better?"

The anger and fight seemed to seep out of him, like a balloon that had been deflated. He stepped back. "Of course not. If I could take it all back, I would. But I can't."

"You can stay away from the Ten Count."

Johnny looked even more miserable than before. "If you think that's what I should do, I will."

"Why should I believe you?"

"Because I'm giving you my word."

Max could have told him his word didn't mean much, but discovered he didn't believe that. The teenager had won his respect for putting the blame on himself and for leaping to Sara's defense.

Max nodded, then returned to the restaurant to face the woman who hadn't trusted him enough to confide in him.

THE DAY HAD RAPIDLY GONE from potentially awful to truly dreadful.

So many things had gone wrong that Sara didn't know which should concern her most. Johnny's guilty role in the sale of the baseball? The possibility that Max might call in the police? Her brother's clear intention to take on men who'd once boxed professionally? Or the knowledge that Max felt betrayed because she hadn't shared what she knew about Johnny?

She sat with her arms crossed, hugging her midsection, wondering as the minutes passed whether she should go after the two men. She was reaching for her wallet to extract some money to pay the bill when she spotted Max returning to the table.

He walked slowly, as though reluctant to return to her. He was unsmiling, looking far different than the lighthearted man who'd necked with her at a red light just the day before. She waited until he settled across from her in the booth before she spoke.

"Please tell me Johnny's not going after the Skaleckys."

"Not anymore, he's not." He spoke with no inflection in his voice.

She longed to reach across the table and cover his hand to communicate how grateful she was but thought better of it. "Thank you."

"Your thanks would sound more sincere if you hadn't tried to cover up what was going on." His jaw was firm, his eyes hard. "You knew Johnny was in on the con and you weren't going to tell me."

She looked away, wondering if there was anything she could say that would mend this rift she'd put between them. "I didn't know that for sure until just now when he admitted it."

"But you suspected."

"Not until I found that piece of paper. I know I should have told you but I wanted to give Johnny a chance to explain first."

The waitress started to approach their table, but Max waved her away. Although people at adjoining tables laughed, talked and ate, it seemed to Sara as though she and Max were alone.

His eyebrow rose in a disbelieving arch. "I find it hard to believe that you would ever have told me about it considering what else you didn't tell me."

The faint scent of the Caesar dressing on her salad reached her nostrils, making her feel sick. She pushed the food off to the side of the table.

"Why did you lie to me, Sara?" His voice sounded

low, tight. "After the nights we spent together, I thought we were past that."

She managed to speak over the misery clogging her throat. "Those nights don't have anything to do with it."

"So you don't have any problem lying to the man you're sleeping with?"

"Of course I do," she retorted, wondering how she could make him understand. She leaned forward, wanting to be closer to him, but feeling as though she put distance between them with every word she spoke. "I didn't tell you because I was afraid you'd automatically assume Johnny was guilty. What was I supposed to do, Max?"

"You were supposed to trust me. You were supposed to be straight with me so I could figure out what was going on."

"I have been straight with you about everything except Johnny's past. The reason I came to you in the first place was to keep him out of jail. You know that."

"What if jail is where he belongs?"

Horror clenched her stomach because this was what she'd feared all along. How could she make him understand what Johnny was really like?

"Let me tell you something about my brother. He's always had a problem with peer pressure. The other three kids who stole the car with him when he was fifteen had records—he was along for the ride.

"After he moved to Florida, my mother told me he had trouble making friends. She thinks that's why he dropped out of school. I'm willing to bet those guys he was with in the music store dared him to take the CDs. He was probably trying to impress them."

Max's expression was so intractable, she could have been talking to a stone. "Running cons is a lot more serious than shoplifting CDs," he said.

"But you heard him, Max. He wasn't in on the second con."

"He was in on the first one."

"And he knows he messed up. He's trying to right his wrong. Ralph won't go to the police if Johnny returns his money. If you do, the cops will automatically be prejudiced against him because of his juvenile record."

Max didn't say anything for a long time. When his gaze met hers, his eyes were sad. "Were you ever going to tell me about that?"

She rubbed at her forehead, feeling a headache coming on. "I don't know. I wanted to, but then the better I got to know you, the more I understood how principled you are."

"I don't follow."

"You think that right is right, wrong is wrong and that people should act a certain way. You're not particularly tolerant when they don't. Look at how quick you've been from the beginning to believe the worst of Larry."

He quirked an eyebrow. "As it turned out, I was right about Larry."

"Yes, but things aren't always that black and white. Sometimes there's a vast gray area."

"You're forgetting something." He leaned forward, hammering home his point. "As an officer of the law, I'm duty bound to stop crime and see criminals punished. I could justify not opening an official investigation into Larry's disappearance because there wasn't any proof of a crime. But now that I've discovered otherwise, I should make it official."

Sara swallowed the panic that rushed up to greet her. "But nobody involved wants to press charges. Ralph Abernathy just wants his money back, and you said that's what the Skaleckys want, too."

"It's not entirely up to them."

"It's up to you, Max. Because if Ralph gets his money back, nobody but you will bring the law into it."

He lapsed into silence. She couldn't tell if her argument had swayed him, so she kept talking. "Why can't you cut Johnny a break? I know he's not a saint, but he's not a villain, either."

"You think I believe that he is?"

"I think you're slow to forgive people's mistakes."

"And I think you're too forgiving. Instead of letting the people you care about suffer the consequences of their actions, you jump in and try to save them. You're doing it now, with Johnny."

"And you're closing your mind to the possibility that he's a kid who made a mistake he wants to atone for," she retorted.

They stared at each other for long moments. The closeness they'd shared the past few days was gone, replaced with a wariness that tore at Sara, a wariness she wasn't sure they'd ever overcome.

"This isn't getting us anywhere, Sara," he said, breaking the silence first. "I can't promise you I won't go to the police, but I did promise you I'd find Larry. And I'd like to do that before the Skalecky brothers manage it."

"Then let's go." She glanced down at the salad

she still hadn't touched. "I seem to have lost my appetite, anyway."

"I'll get the waitress to box it up," he said, ready to signal for the waitress. "Then I'll drive you back to school."

"I'm not going back to school," she said. "I'm going to help you figure out where Larry is."

MAX DROPPED HIS HAND and leaned back in the booth, careful to keep his expression neutral. He was still hurt and angry at Sara for lying to him, but damn if he didn't admire her determination. "And how do you propose to do that?"

"Surely you've heard the saying about two heads being better than one. Tell what you're thinking and I'll be your sounding board. Maybe I can help you come up with some theories."

Max hesitated before answering. He'd worked with partners before but operated best alone. With Sara, there was another variable. He may be angry with her, but he still wanted to keep her in a bubble, safe from harm.

"Go ahead," she urged, and he figured it wouldn't hurt to hear what she had to say.

He got his thoughts in order. "I think Larry was pretty deep in debt to that loan shark. I think he tried another con because the money from the sale of the baseball didn't cover his entire debt."

The scent from the cheeseburger Johnny had ordered reached his nostrils, alerting Max that despite everything he was hungry. He picked it up and took a bite, thinking while he chewed.

"Go on," Sara prodded.

He finished chewing and swallowed. "I think

Larry's off somewhere trying to raise the money. If he comes back to town without it, he knows the Skaleckys will be waiting for him."

Larry probably also knew that the Skaleckys would be waiting for him regardless, but would go easier on him if he came back with the cash.

"The question is how is Larry going to get the money? I made a second round of calls to his friends and family. No one admitted lending it to him."

"Then maybe he's trying to win it back." Sara worried a strand of hair between two fingers. "Atlantic City is only a couple hours drive from Baltimore. Larry could be there."

Max thought about that as he chewed and swallowed another bite of cheeseburger. "Maybe, but I don't buy it. Larry's a lot of things, but stupid isn't one of them. Unless gambling's become a real problem for him, I can't see him leaving something this important to luck."

"Then where do you think he is?"

That was the puzzler. If Larry hadn't solicited his friends for a loan and if he wasn't in Atlantic City, where was he? What would Max do if he were in Larry's position?

Sell something, probably.

But Max had been inside Larry's apartment. Although Larry lived beyond his means, he'd be hard pressed to come up with anything that would bring in enough cash to pay off a sizeable debt. Think, Max told himself. What did Larry have of value?

"The sculpture," he answered aloud.

"Excuse me?"

"The sculpture, the one Larry nicknamed Barbarellen." The more he thought about it, the more sense it made. "Where does he usually keep it?"

"On the mantle in his living room. Why?"

"Because when we were in his apartment, he didn't have it on display. I looked over that place pretty good. If it had been there, I would have seen it." He thought for a moment. "How much do you think it's worth?"

"Quite a bit, but Larry wouldn't sell it. It's his prized possession."

"Larry values his face more than a sculpture. If he knows the Skaleckys are looking for him, he'd re-think hanging on to some bits of bronze."

"But where would he sell it?"

Max's brain rewound to the previous afternoon, when Larry's weird little neighbor had claimed that Larry had been very interested in how he made his living.

"Do you have a computer?" he asked Sara.

She nodded. "Doesn't everybody?"

"Then let's go." Max threw some bills down on the table and headed for the door, leaving a half-finished cheeseburger and Sara's salad.

Sara's voice came from behind him. "What does my computer have to do with anything?"

"I want to see if anybody's advertised a sculpture called Barbarellen on eBay."

11

SARA STOOD BEHIND Max at the computer in her bedroom, wanting to believe that Max accepting her help constituted a step forward in their relationship but knowing that their problems were only on hold.

Once they dealt with them, she might never see him again.

She shoved aside the thought and watched as Max typed "Barbarellen" into the eBay search engine. Not a single hit. He tried again, this time typing "sculpture" and coming up with more than twenty-four hundred sculptures for sale.

He clicked the mouse and a screen appeared displaying some of them. There were sculptures made of metal, bronze, marble, wood and assorted other materials. Some were created to titillate, such as the erotic bronze of a couple making love. Others to draw attention, like the five-foot-tall elephant made from car bumpers.

You name it, an eBay seller was peddling it.

"It's going to take a while to go through all these entries," Max said.

"Not necessarily." Sara took control of the mouse and had the computer list the highest priced items first. "If the sculpture's valuable, it'll be among those listed first."

Only the top fifty items had asking prices of more than a few thousand dollars. Max scrolled through them, but none were Barbarellen.

"Maybe we're too late," he said, frustration evident in his voice. "If Larry already sold the sculpture, we've struck out."

"Let me try one more thing." Sara's breasts brushed against Max when she leaned over him to reclaim the mouse. A wave of remembered sensations struck her, which she tried valiantly to ignore while she moved the mouse to the left-hand side of the page and checked the box next to "completed items."

"How did you know that was there?" Max's breath was soft and sweet against her cheek.

"You'll laugh."

"No, I won't."

"I once bid on a Buffy the Vampire Slayer action figure and wanted to make sure I didn't pay too much."

"Why Buffy?" She'd expected amusement to lace his voice but instead heard curiosity.

She thought for a moment because she'd never before examined her partiality toward the character. "Because she never hesitates to put her life on the line, especially if somebody's messing with one of her friends."

Before Max could question her further, she clicked the mouse button and sorted the items so that the most expensive ones would be listed first. The second item to appear was a stick figure holding up a barbell.

"Eureka," she said.

Max took over control of the mouse, clicking to the item's accompanying description. The heading read, "Lift your status in the community by displaying

this clever commentary on the strength of a woman
by a renowned sculptor."

He scrolled down to a photo of the sculpture,
which Sara thought caught its whimsical nature.
"That's the sculpture. Now let's see who bought it
and for how much."

Max whistled, and Sara would have done the
same if she knew how. A buyer whose eBay ID was
TheOddestOfEnds had bid twenty thousand for the
sculpture, which was to be paid by money order. The
bidding had ended two days ago.

"I need to find out where that money order was
sent, but user IDs are private," Max said. "By the
time I convince someone in authority to give me a
name, it could be too late."

"Let's switch places." Sara slipped into the chair
when he rose. It was still warm from his body. "The-
OddestOfEnds sounds like it could be a store. The
user might have created an About Me page."

She clicked through layers of pages until she
found the information she sought. TheOddest-
OfEnds, just as she'd suspected, was a store that sold
knickknacks. The owner had not only listed a Los
Angeles address but a phone number.

Max picked up the phone beside the computer
and dialed before she could suggest it.

"It's an answering machine," he told her, then
muttered. "Would you believe the store's open six
days a week but not on Wednesdays? I get that they
probably do more business on weekends, but why
not take off Monday? Why Wednesday?"

"What now?" she asked when he hung up.

"You have a lab this afternoon, right? I'll drive
you back to school."

She hadn't expected him to thank her for her help but neither had she anticipated that he'd try to get rid of her.

He started toward the door, no doubt expecting her to follow but disappointment kept her glued to the computer chair. He turned and looked back at her. "You coming?"

"Maybe there's something else I can do."

He shook his head. "I can handle it from here."

He looked cool, calm, composed... and remote. Part of the fault for the distance that had sprung between them could be traced to her lie, but she thought it was more than that.

She got up and slowly walked across the room to his side. When she reached him, she still felt as though he were far away.

He'd accepted her help in figuring out what Larry was up to only because she'd practically forced herself on him, but the bottom line was still the same.

He didn't need her. And she didn't think he ever would.

MAX PHONED HIS PARTNER at the FBI as soon as he saw Sara safely disappear into the nursing school. Dan Davis picked up after the first ring.

"You must miss me," Dan said. "This is two calls in two days."

"Don't you have a brother who's a cop in California?"

"Hello to you, too," Dan said. "Jenny says to tell you she still thinks you need a girlfriend and she can fix you up with a woman in her office when you get back to town. And, yeah, my brother's a cop in California."

"What city in California?"

"Man, you really need to work on your social skills," Dan complained. "Los Angeles."

"Can you get him on the phone and have him track down the owner of this store?" Max rattled off the address Sara had pulled up from eBay. "The store's closed Wednesdays, but I need somebody to talk to the owner today."

"What do you want from the owner of this place?"

"He bought a sculpture on eBay a few days ago, and I need to know where he sent the payment."

Dan didn't say anything for a few moments. "Does this have something to do with those men you wanted me to run background checks on? I've got to tell you, buddy, I'm worried. It's not like you to do things off the books."

Dan was right. It wasn't like him. Neither was it like him to get phone records without a court order. But he'd done it because Sara was counting on him.

"These are special circumstances," he told Dan.

Dan whistled. "Then it must be important."

"I wouldn't ask for your help if it weren't."

"Then I'll call my brother and twist his arm until he agrees to do this. I'll give him your cell number so he can call you back directly."

"Thanks," Max said. "And Dan?"

"Yeah?"

"Tell your wife I appreciate the thought but I don't need her to set me up."

Within the hour, Dan's brother called Max directly with the information. The owner of the Oddest of Ends was a man named Charley Warren, who had mailed the money order to a hotel on Delaware's Bethany Beach but had yet to receive the sculpture.

Max thanked him and quickly got the hotel receptionist on the line. Larry Brunell, she said, had checked out that morning.

The next step was a no-brainer. He needed to camp out at the Ten Count. The brothers should already be at the gym, and Larry could be headed there.

Even if Larry returned the money in full, the combination spelled trouble. There was no guarantee the Skaleckys would let him off the hook before they roughed him up.

No matter what Larry had done, he didn't deserve that.

He checked his watch. Sara's lab wasn't due to end for another forty-five minutes, but he punched her number into his cell phone anyway to warn her that Larry could be on his way back to Baltimore.

He didn't want Sara anywhere near the other man until the matter was resolved.

SARA CONCENTRATED on flicking her wrist so that the needle penetrated the entire way into the rolled-up bandage masquerading as a human arm. The make-believe person who should have been attached to the arm was diabetic, the needle filled with saline instead of insulin.

The cell phone she'd dropped into the deep pocket of her long white lab coat vibrated. She flinched and the needle penetrated only halfway.

"Sorry," she said to the bandage, then rolled her eyes.

"Sara?" Professor Donagal, a white-haired woman with a bedside manner that would have rivaled Florence Nightingale's, sidled up to her. "What's the problem?"

Sara's cell phone vibrated again, eliciting an audible buzz. The professor's brows drew together in disapproval. "You should have turned the cell phone off, Sara. They're not allowed in lab."

Sara pulled the needle out of the bandage and recapped it without sticking herself, a minor victory. "I know, Professor, but I really need to take this call. It's an emergency."

Professor Donagal's expression softened at the magic word. Nurses knew all about emergencies. She nodded toward the door. "Then go."

Sara rushed into the hall, dug the phone from her lab-coat pocket and paused. The number on display wasn't the same one Max had given her for his cell phone, but she supposed he could be calling from a landline. She clicked the phone on. "Hello."

"Sara, it's Larry."

Her mouth dropped open, her mind raced and her heart rate accelerated. "Larry! Are you all right?"

"I'm fine."

She leaned against the wall, glad classes were in session and the hallway was quiet so she could figure out what was going on. "But where have you been? We've been looking all over for you."

"Why?" He sounded guarded.

"I think you know why. Johnny's in trouble. Ralph Abernathy is threatening to go to the police if he doesn't get the rest of his money back."

"Why would he want his money back?"

Sara's relief that he was physically unharmed gave way to anger. "Don't play dumb with me, Larry. I know that you and Johnny conned that poor old man. I also know about the lottery ticket and the grandmother of those boxers."

"You know about the Skalecky brothers?" He sounded wary.

"Thanks to Max. He put the pieces together after Rocky Skalecky started hanging around the Rusty Nail."

"Max Dolinger?"

"Yes. He was visiting Maryland and I asked for his help." She stopped abruptly. She couldn't afford to tell Larry too much and have him disappear again, not when he could still prevent Johnny from going to jail. Besides, he was the one who owed her explanations. "Where are you? I didn't recognize the number."

"I picked up one of those cell phones that uses a prepaid phone card," he said, which didn't entirely answer her question. "You're at nursing school, right?"

"Right," she said warily, then asked again. "Where are you?"

"Waiting in my car outside the building."

"Waiting for what?"

"For you. Hear me out, Sara. I know you have a right to be angry with me and I know I have a lot to apologize for, but I'm in a jam and I really need your help. Could you meet me at the car? Please?"

Sara remembered that Max had claimed she was a sucker for anyone in need. But this was different. She needed something from Larry, too. If he didn't hand over the money he and Johnny owed Ralph Abernathy, Johnny would almost certainly go to jail.

What harm could there be in meeting Larry in broad daylight? Especially when she'd call Max and let him know exactly what was going on.

"I'll be right there," she said.

Max drummed his fingers on the steering wheel as he listened to the incessant buzz of a busy signal and waited for Sara to put her other caller on hold and come onto the line.

The busy signal buzzed on, forcing him to face the fact that not all cell-phone plans included call waiting. His didn't. He ended the call, immediately hit Redial but got the same blasted busy signal.

Who the hell could Sara be talking to? She was supposed to be in the middle of a lab, not chatting on the phone.

Even as he asked himself the question, he acknowledged that there could be any number of innocent answers. Her class could be taking a short break. She could have accidentally depressed a button and not realized the phone was on. She could have lent the thing to someone.

But he couldn't accept any of those answers because the knot in his gut told him something was wrong. He maneuvered the car into a U-turn, heading away from the Ten Count and toward the nursing school.

He wasted precious time circling the building looking for an elusive parking spot. A young woman whose waist-length black hair swung when she walked remotely unlocked the door of a white Honda, and he flicked on his turn signal.

His cell rang before he could pull into the spot, the number display identifying Sara as the caller. Heaving a sigh of relief, he depressed the button. "Hello."

"Max. I'm so glad I finally reached you."

"Reached me? I've been trying to get in touch with you." He didn't give her a chance to respond. What he had to say was too important to wait. "Listen. I think Larry is on his way back to Baltimore and this thing is about to come to a head. I want you to stay out of the way until it's straightened out."

"I can't," she said and he nearly groaned aloud at her stubbornness. Before he could make another stab at convincing her to stay put, she added, "I'm helping Larry straighten it out."

His heart thudded so hard he could feel the vibrations. "Please tell me you're still at school."

"Don't be angry, Max, but I'm with Larry. We've worked it all out. After I deliver what he owes to the Skaleckys, he's going to give the money back to Ralph Abernathy."

A half-dozen vicious curse words leaped to mind but Max swallowed them because Larry was the one who deserved his wrath. How could he put Sara in danger like that?

Max rocketed past the empty parking place and veered into the left-turn lane at the next stoplight. Reining in his anger, he said, "Sara, listen to me. I'm heading to the Ten Count right now. Whatever you do, don't get out of the car."

"But the Skaleckys won't hurt me. I didn't take the money from their grandmother."

"How do they know you weren't in on the con? These are not choirboys, Sara. Brad Skalecky did time. Rocky was a champion boxer. You and Larry need to turn around and get out of there."

While she relayed the message to Larry, he waited impatiently for the light to turn green, then sped through the intersection.

"Okay. We're going to turn around," she said.

Before the air could resume its unimpeded flow

through his lungs, he heard Larry swear. "What's wrong?" Max asked.

"The car behind us is blocking us. Oh, no."

"What?"

"It's that guy who's been hanging around the pub, and he doesn't look happy. I think…"

The line went dead. With fingers that shook, Max put another call through to Sara's cell phone. Nothing.

His heart pounded, the blood rushing to his brain making it hard to think. But then his training took over. He tossed the phone onto the passenger seat and concentrated on driving to the Ten Count.

On a normal day, he could make the drive from the nursing school to the gym in about ten minutes. With his heart racing and the tires on his car screeching, he got there in five.

He scanned the lot, wishing he'd asked Sara what kind of car Larry drove. Then he saw it. A black Mustang effectively hemmed into a parking spot by a dusty pickup truck parked at a right angle to its bumper.

He drove closer and spotted three men not far from the blockade. Two of them—one short, the other tall, both muscular—stood on either side of a third, golden-haired man, who from his hand gestures appeared to be trying to talk himself out of getting pummeled.

The boxing brothers had Larry surrounded, but where was Sara? He saw her next, standing off to the side of the cluster of men but not as far away as Max would have preferred. Hell, Alaska wouldn't be far enough away.

Rocky Skalecky charged Larry at about the same

time Max hit the brake. The boxer planted his feet, pulled back his arm, gained power from his legs, hips and shoulders and connected the knuckles of his right hand with Larry's face.

Max opened the car door in time to hear Larry howl with pain. Max winced. He didn't believe in street justice. No matter what Larry had done, he didn't deserve this.

Brad Skalecky advanced on the cowering Larry from the other direction. Sara rushed into the fray, stepping in front of Larry and temporarily stopping Brad's charge. The breath in Max's lungs seized.

"Get out of my way," the taller brother bellowed, his face reddened with anger.

"No." Sara lifted her chin, but her show of defiance didn't impress Brad. He resumed his charge.

Max didn't think; he reacted. Withdrawing his Glock from his ankle holster with a fluid motion, he trained it on the boxer. "FBI. Stop or I'll shoot."

He'd never be able to justify the use of deadly force, but the threat wasn't idle. Brad Skalecky might not be carrying but his fist could do Sara serious damage.

Playing by the rules no longer mattered to Max. All that mattered was Sara.

Brad Skalecky stopped. Sara looked at Max like he was some kind of hero. Larry moaned. Rocky Skalecky raised his hands in the air.

"What's the freaking FBI doing here?" Rocky Skalecky said. "This is private, man. We don't want no trouble. All we want is the money this lowlife stole from our grandma."

"I told you I'd give it to you. You didn't have to hit me." Larry said through the screen of his hands.

His voice sounded nasal and wet. "I think you broke my nose."

"Where's the money?" Max asked roughly, and Larry pointed a shaky finger at Sara.

Max lowered his gun but didn't holster it. As he passed Larry, he muttered, "You're lucky I don't hit you myself."

Before Sara could move, Max took the envelope from her. Being careful to keep himself between her and the two boxers, he handed the money to Rocky Skalecky, who tore open the envelope and counted the bills.

"Is it all there?" his brother asked gruffly.

"Of course it's all there. Plus the interest you insisted on." Larry sounded as though he were about to cry. He'd removed his shirt and had it wadded up at his nose to stop the bleeding.

Brad "Bubba" Skalecky glared at him. "You're lucky we didn't insist on breaking your legs, you no-good son of a bitch."

Larry shrank back. "I wouldn't talk to me like that if you don't want me to press charges against you for breaking my nose."

"How 'bout we press charges against you for being a scumbag?" Rocky Skalecky roared.

"Nobody's pressing any charges," Sara said firmly.

"That's right. He got what was coming to him." Rocky Skalecky gestured at the cowering Larry, then held up the money. "And we got what was coming to us. We don't want no trouble. Not with the FBI."

The mention of the bureau reminded Max that this case had gone well beyond the realm of unofficial but the truth was that the police would have a hard time making arrests stick if nobody was willing to press charges.

"If you don't want any trouble with me, stay away from the Rusty Nail." Max got in the taller Skalecky brother's face and glowered at him. "One more thing. If you dare come near Sara or her house again, I'll come after you myself."

"It wasn't her I was after." He pointed a thick finger at Larry. "It was him."

"Just tell him you'll stay away from the lady, Brad," Rocky urged.

"I'll stay away," he muttered. "But if that joker messes with our grandma again, we'll rip off his nose and stuff it in his mouth."

"Fair enough," Max said.

"What's fair about giving them permission to mutilate me?" Larry complained.

"Then it's settled, and our business is done." Rocky took his brother by the arm and pointed him in the direction of the gym. Brad walked away, casting a wary look back over his shoulder at Max, while Rocky moved the pickup truck.

"I've got to go to the hospital," Larry said.

"Put a cap on it, Larry. You're lucky I didn't break your nose myself for getting Sara stuck in the middle of this. Now tell me where the rest of the money is."

"In the glove compartment," Larry said, nodding toward his car. "But you don't have to act like I'm hiding it. I told Sara I'd give it back, and that's what I'm going to do."

"No, you're not," Max said. "I am."

Max went to the car and retrieved a still-thick envelope of cash from the glove compartment. He counted out the seventy-five hundred Larry owed Ralph Abernathy, vaguely surprised that it was all there.

"You're not out of the woods yet, Larry," he said after slamming the car door shut. "Ralph Abernathy could still go to the police."

"Sara said he wouldn't if he got his money back."

Max walked over to his former friend, crouched down and brought his face inches from the other man's, whispering so Sara couldn't overhear. "He will if I convince him to."

"Jeez, man," Larry said. "I thought we were friends."

"We used to be friends, Larry. There's a difference." Max turned from Larry and nodded to Sara. "Let's get out of here."

"You can't go and leave me here," Larry protested loudly. "What about my nose?"

Sara hesitated, leveling an anxious glance at Larry. "I should take a look at his nose."

Max held on to his temper, but just barely. "Why, Sara? The guy's brought you nothing but trouble. Hell, he's even gotten your brother in trouble. You don't owe him a damn thing."

The only sound was the slight song of the wind as it blew through the parking lot until Larry piped up.

"I think my face has gone numb," Larry complained. "I feel tingling. This is serious, man. Sara, will you take me to the hospital? Please?"

Sara put a hand on Max's arm. "I know I don't owe him anything, Max. And believe me, I am angry at him. But I'm studying to be a nurse. I can't just leave him there like that."

Max released a short breath and made one more stab at salvaging a relationship he already feared was beyond saving. "It's his nose that's broken, not his foot. Let him drive himself."

"Sara." Larry had taken a couple steps closer to them. "Please, can we go?"

Sara's troubled eyes cut from Max to Larry and back again. Then she made her choice. "I'm sorry, Max, but I've got to drive Larry to the hospital. He needs me."

Max felt as if a knife were digging into his heart as Sara released his arm and walked past him to where Larry stood with his shirt covering his nose. She gently took his bare arm and walked with him to the car, making sure he was settled in the passenger seat before getting behind the steering wheel.

Logically Max knew that Sara didn't intend to get back together with Larry, but that hardly mattered.

She'd claimed to be leaving with Larry because he needed her. Someone, it seemed, always needed her. Someone always would need her.

Why hadn't it ever dawned on her that Max was the one who needed her most of all?

12

THE BRIGHT OVERHEAD LIGHTS cast the hospital waiting room into stark focus, illuminating the human drama.

A young woman in the chair across the aisle doubled over in pain while her male companion rubbed her back. A few chairs away slumped a teenage boy whose complexion had gone almost as pale as the white of a nurse's uniform. A small child sitting on his mother's lap tugged on his ear, crying copious tears.

Sara had to bite down on her lower lip so she wouldn't offer to try to treat their ailments. Since she was only in her first month of nursing school, she doubted the higher-ups at Johns Hopkins would condone that.

"I can't believe they wouldn't take me right away. Can't they see I'm suffering?" Larry had his head tipped back, an ice pack on his nose.

Sara took a good look at his perfectly cut hair, his completely symmetrical features and his tall, lean body. The receptionist had found the short-sleeved, V-neck pullover top of some hospital scrubs for him to wear. It was too big and green wasn't his color, but even that couldn't detract from the fact that Larry Brunell was a hottie.

Is that why she'd wasted so much time on him? No, she wasn't that shallow.

Adversity was bringing out the worst in Larry, but most of the time he was as charming as a prince. His charm wasn't the reason she'd hung around him either, though.

To get to the bottom of the mystery, all she had to do was look at the reason she'd driven him to the hospital. Larry, like most of the men she'd dated, was needy.

"A broken nose isn't the end of the world, Larry," she said with more patience than she felt. "Look around. Almost everyone here needs medical attention worse than you do."

He shot her a pained look. "Whose side are you on? I've been through a lot, Sara."

The stress she'd been under erupted in a spate of words. "You've been through a lot? That's rich, Larry. You left town and everyone else had to deal with your problems. You don't have any right to complain."

"So now you want me to apologize for looking out for myself? The Skalecky brothers were after me. Don't you get that?"

She stared at him, amazed that he could be so self-centered. He seemed to have no concept of the danger he'd brought to her door. And why hadn't she had the good sense to slam her door shut on him anyway? She'd broken up with him, yet still wanted to fix him.

She closed her eyes, thinking about how Max had asked her not to drive Larry to the hospital, picturing how pained he'd looked when she'd insisted that she had to.

When she opened her eyes, she felt as though she were seeing things clearly for the first time. Larry hadn't meant anything to her for a very long time. She could have refused to drive him to the hospital. She should have refused.

"I need to go," she announced abruptly and stood up.

Larry lifted his head. His nose had stopped bleeding, but discoloration had already started to set in. "You can't mean that, Sara. You've always been there for me, and now I'm hurting. I need you to stay with me."

"What you need is to start taking responsibility for your own actions," Sara said. "I can't keep being your savior, Larry. I won't be."

His eyes narrowed. "Does this have something to do with Max? Because I'm telling you right now he'll break your heart. That's the kind of guy he is."

"He's the best man I know."

Larry made a disbelieving sound. "You won't think so much of him if he convinces Ralph Abernathy to tell the police what your brother and I did."

"He wouldn't do that," Sara retorted.

"Why? Because of you? Think again, Sara. Max would turn in his own grandmother if she did something wrong. He won't hesitate to turn in your brother."

"That's just wild speculation on your part."

"I wish it were," Larry said, sounding tired. "But Max told me he could convince the old man to press charges."

"He could," Sara said. "But he won't."

Without a backward glance, she walked out of the

automatic doors of the emergency room. The sky had been cloudy and threatening when she'd first approached Max for help but now it shone brightly.

She recognized the irony in that. Because despite her heated denials, she feared that Max might do exactly what Larry said he would and go to the police.

LARRY BRUNELL DESERVED TO BE in jail.

The knowledge weighed down Max's steps as he walked up the sidewalk to his grandparents' house, just as the wad of cash he carried caused his pocket to sag.

The Skaleckys had refused to press charges against Larry, but Max felt sure he could convince Ralph Abernathy to do so. Persuading the old man that Larry needed to pay for what he'd done wouldn't be too difficult, especially because Abernathy would get his money back regardless of what happened.

There was only one problem with the scenario: Johnny Reynolds would have to pay, too.

That wouldn't have bothered Max a week ago. His thinking on the matter would have been clearcut. Johnny had made a mistake. Johnny should be punished for it.

He wasn't all that sure why that scenario bothered him now, but he did know that indecision over how to proceed had so far kept him from phoning Abernathy and setting up a meet.

Max climbed the still-creaky porch steps, unlocked the front door and walked into the unremitting silence.

He'd thought the house quiet without his grandparents there, but it had been a peaceful quiet. Without Sara, the silence was almost unbearable.

His cell phone rang, and his first thought was of Sara. But a quick check of the number told him she wasn't the caller. His shoulders sagging, he clicked on the phone and said hello.

"Max. This is Irene Jenkins." The real-estate agent. "I called to see what kind of progress you've been making. How does the house look?"

When he'd pulled into the driveway, he'd noticed that the yard looked green and tidy. The roofers who had come this morning to replace sagging tiles had done a credible job. Cardboard boxes no longer cluttered the front porch, the charity having picked up his donations. Through the sliding glass door leading to the back of the house, Max could see that the men he'd hired to pressure-wash the deck had made it sparkle.

"The house looks great," he said.

"Excellent. Now all we need is for you to be at my office tomorrow morning at nine to sign the papers."

Tomorrow was Thursday. Max's return flight to Texas was on Friday. His original intention had been to leave the real-estate agent to sell the house and he'd take care of the details of the sale long distance, so he wouldn't have to come back to Maryland. The idea of severing ties with the area forever hadn't bothered him.

But that had been a lifetime ago, before Sara had come to him for help. Sara, who in this very house had fervently insisted he wasn't responsible for the sins of his parents.

Sara, who'd tried to tell him that black and white mixed together made gray.

"Max? Are you still there?"

"I'm still here, Irene. But about that appointment tomorrow morning. I need to cancel."

"Cancel?" The pitch of her voice rose. "But you can't. You're leaving soon. If we don't meet tomorrow, when would we meet?"

"I'll have to get back to you on that," he said and hung up, even though she was still protesting.

Talking to the realtor ranked far down on his list of things to do because suddenly his course of action had become crystal clear, starting with the phone call that would get the ball rolling.

He called information, asked for the phone number of The Coffee Ground and had the computer automatically dial the number. A moment later, Sara's brother came on the line.

"Johnny, this is Max Dolinger. You and I need to see a man about a baseball."

WEDNESDAY NIGHT at the Rusty Nail Pub was busier than usual, thanks to an extended happy hour that ended at 9:00 p.m. instead of seven.

Sara usually didn't have time for anything except filling drink orders and picking up empty glasses, but today her mind moved faster than her feet.

Had Max made good on his threat to convince Ralph Abernathy to press charges?

She'd tried contacting Johnny several times that afternoon to find out the answer. She hadn't been able to reach him, which probably meant he'd forgotten to charge his cell-phone battery again.

She hadn't tried phoning Max.

She was returning to the bar after delivering long, cold ones to a couple so in love they'd barely looked up, when Trixie grabbed her arm.

"Trixie," she said in surprise. "Did you just get here?"

"Five minutes ago and I already have news," Trixie whispered and pulled her over to the only relatively private place in the bar, a short hallway leading to the restrooms. "The phone was ringing when I got here. Guess who it was?"

She didn't wait for Sara's guess, but plunged ahead, her voice never rising above a hush. "Larry. I told him I'd get you on the phone, but he wanted me to relay a message. Get this. He said he can come into work tomorrow but not tonight because his nose is broken."

"I know," Sara said.

"What do you mean you know?"

"I was there when it got broken," she said and proceeded to tell a wide-eyed Trixie a shortened version of what had happened. She ended with the possibility that Johnny could still be in trouble with the police.

"Oh, man," Trixie said. "I always suspected Larry was a snake, but I can't believe Max turned out to be one, too."

"Don't say that," Sara said. "Max is the complete opposite of a snake."

"But you just said he might convince that man to press charges. If he does, he'll be responsible for putting your brother in jail."

Trixie's rationale wasn't any different than Sara's had been, but suddenly it sounded all wrong.

"Max wouldn't be responsible," Sara said, feeling as though she were looking at the situation clearly for the first time. "Johnny would. Max can't be faulted for listening to his conscience and doing what he thinks is right."

"I don't get it," Trixie said, shaking her head. "Where's the woman who would do anything to protect her brother?"

Sara brought a hand to her head as reality struck her. "She fell in love with a man she just now realized she shouldn't have asked to compromise his principles."

"You're in love with Max?"

"Desperately in love with him. He's such a good man, Trixie. That's part of the reason I love him." She clutched her friend's hand. "Do you think he'll ever forgive me for what I asked him to do?"

"You could ask him yourself." Trixie took her by the shoulders and turned her so she faced the front of the pub. "He just walked through the door."

Because Max was a good three or four inches taller than most of the other people in the bar, it was easy to spot him. He was dressed in casual FBI chic again: the short hair, the crisp-looking pants, the conservative polo shirt.

Sara stared, drinking in the sight of him like some of the pub's customers were downing beers. The strength of his character showed in every angle and plane of his face.

"Go talk to him," Trixie said, giving her a little push. "I'll cover for you."

"But it's so crowded."

"If the customers get thirsty enough, they'll go to the bar and order their drinks themselves. Now go."

Sara went. Max hadn't ventured any deeper into the bar, but remained near the entrance, his eyes combing the interior. She prepared herself to feel a frosty blast when his gaze landed on her, but the corners of his mouth slowly lifted into a smile so warm that her heart melted.

She kept walking and he met her halfway, somewhere between the corner of the bar and one of the front tables.

His eyes ran over her face as though it were years instead of hours since he'd last seen her. "I've got something to tell you," he said.

"Me first." She took his hand and tugged so he followed her from the pub into the fading early evening light.

O'Donnell Square would be a better place to have this conversation, but she couldn't wait for the time it took to cross the street to tell him what was in her heart. So she led him two storefronts away to the entrance of a shoe-repair shop that had closed an hour ago.

"I'm sorry," she blurted out. "I've made a mess of things between us."

She still held his hand, and he squeezed hers. "No. I'm the one who's sorry. I should have understood why you needed to go to the hospital with Larry. I should have known that's who you are."

She gaped at him, surprised by his apology when she'd been in the wrong. She never should have left Max to go with Larry. Max was the man she loved, the man she needed as much as the blood running through her veins and pumping into her heart.

"But you were right about me, Max," Sara said. "I can't be everybody's savior. And yes, I know I won't always be able to resist the urge to jump in and help when it's not my place. But I will be able to resist when the person in trouble is Larry."

Max's dark eyebrows drew together. "Exactly what happened at the hospital?"

"Larry was being Larry, trying to make me feel like I had some obligation to him. And why not? I'd been trying to help him get out of one scrape or another since I met him."

"You cared about him."

"I'm not sure that's true. I think I started going out with him because I thought he needed me. What I cared about was helping him. But it hit me in the emergency room that I couldn't help everybody and it was past time Larry started helping himself."

Although relieved she'd gotten that off her chest, she had a tougher confession to make. "But that's not what I was apologizing about."

"It's not?"

She shook her head. "I was apologizing for asking you to go against what you believed. I shouldn't have done that, Max. I should have come clean about Johnny's past right at the start."

"But you thought I'd go to the police if I had all the facts."

"Then I should have accepted that," she said. "I do accept it. I like who you are, Max. I like your sense of honor, your sense of decency, your willingness to do the right thing.

"Don't get me wrong. I still don't want you to turn

in my brother. I still believe that he's sorry and that he's telling the truth about walking the straight and narrow from here on out. But I'll understand if you feel you have to bring the police into it."

"That was quite a speech," he said and grinned at her. "But now I have something to show you."

This time he was the one who took her hand. He walked with her down the block, stopping at his car. He took the keys from his pocket, unlocked it remotely and left to get something from the passenger seat.

When he straightened, he called out, "Here, catch."

He tossed her something small and white, and she caught it on its downward arc. A baseball. But not just any baseball. She turned it over, finding a signature scrawled across it.

Eight letters strung together in cursive writing, worth thousands if Babe Ruth had put them there, nothing if he hadn't. He hadn't.

"This is Johnny's baseball." Her brows drew together. "What are you doing with it?"

"Johnny and I went to see Ralph Abernathy this afternoon to return the rest of his money. He didn't want the ball anymore, and neither did Johnny."

He reached into his pocket and unfolded an official-looking piece of paper. "This is the fake certificate of authentication. If the police got hold of this, they could have used it as evidence against your brother."

Crumpling the paper into a ball, he tossed it into a nearby trash can.

"But why did you throw that away?" Sara asked, clutching the baseball so tightly her hand hurt. "I thought you were going to talk Abernathy into pressing charges."

"It turned out I didn't need to. Abernathy had decided to do that on his own. Turned out he'd gotten angrier and angrier when he thought about how Johnny and Larry had swindled him."

"So what happened?"

"I convinced him Johnny was a good kid who'd made a mistake and deserved a second chance," he said. "I couldn't make the same assurances about Larry. But I told Abernathy I had contacts at the Baltimore PD and that I'd get somebody to keep tabs on him. If he doesn't straighten out, I promised to make it a personal mission to see Larry behind bars."

"You did all that?" She tried to make it all compute but couldn't. "Why?"

"Partly because you made me see the light." He smiled. "You were right, Sara. Not everything in life is cut-and-dried. People make mistakes. And when they're truly sorry for what they've done and want to change, we need to make allowances for that.

"I was too inflexible to see that before. If I hadn't fallen in love with you, I might never have realized that."

He covered her lips with three fingers. Cars passed by on the street and pedestrians walked on the sidewalk, but she could only see and hear Max.

"Before you say anything, let me state my case. I am a good man, Sara. You said so yourself. I know you probably think this thing between us is happening too fast, but it doesn't feel that way to me. I know I've wanted you for a long time, since the wedding, when I first saw you. And I'll be good to you, Sara.

You're never going to find another man who loves you as much as I do."

She gently removed his fingers from her lips, but didn't let them go. "Are you trying to talk me into loving you?" she asked incredulously.

His face actually flushed, and he looked adorably embarrassed. "Well, yeah, I guess I am."

She smiled. "Then you don't have to bother, because I already do."

There was a split-second delay before he grinned like a kid who'd just been told he could have all the candy he could eat, then gathered her to him for a kiss full of passion and promise. They were both breathless when he finally drew back.

She touched his cheek and waited for her brains to unscramble because there was something else she needed to tell him.

"I've been so busy worrying about what everybody else needed that I haven't taken care of my own needs," she said. "I need *you*, Max. And as long as you love me, I can accept that you don't need me."

"Don't need you?" His brows drew together and his mouth gaped open. "Where did you get that idea?"

"From you," she said, trying to convey that she could live with the knowledge. "From the way you try to do everything yourself, even from the way you make love. You're… so contained."

"Only because I was afraid you'd run if you saw how much I wanted you."

"There's that word again," Sara said sadly. "Want. It's different from need."

"I do want you, Sara. I'll never deny that, but I need you as much as I need to breathe, maybe more."

He took her by the shoulders, gave her a gentle shake. "Don't you get it? I not only need you to believe in me, I need you to love me."

Her eyes grew wide as the truth in his declaration penetrated. He'd been alone in the true sense of the word since his grandparents had died, but he'd been lonely long before then.

"You have my love," she said solemnly, then stopped him when he would have kissed her. "But we have so much to work out. Already I can't stand the thought of you going back to Texas."

"I have to. My job's there."

She made a split decision. "Then I'm coming with you."

"Oh, no you're not."

"But I thought…" She pursed her lips together, tried again. Was it possible that she'd misunderstood him, that all he was in the market for was a long-distance love affair? "I thought you wanted us to be together."

"Not at the expense of your education," he said firmly.

"I can go to nursing school anywhere."

"You can't go to a prestigious nursing school anywhere. I won't let you make that big of a sacrifice for me."

She implored him to understand. "But nursing school won't mean anything if we can't be together."

"I want us to be together, too. So tell me how this sounds." He ran his hands through her hair and over her face, as though he couldn't stop touching her. "I'll keep my grandparents' house and put in for a transfer.

"The special agent in charge of the FBI's field office in Baltimore initially wanted me to be assigned here because of my ties to the city. If I call him, he'll go to bat for me."

Sara's heart swelled with love for him. "You'll do that for me?"

"Only if you do something for me, too. Quit your job at Rusty's and find another one that relates to nursing."

"Okay," she said. "But what do you need me to do for *you*?"

He didn't hesitate before he answered. "I need for you to love me."

She smiled up at him, pulled his head down to hers and that's exactly what she did.

If you enjoyed TO THE MAX,
make sure you catch…
Blaze #179
BORN TO BE BAD
by Crystal Green
Available this month.

Deep undercover. That's how far tabloid reporter
Gemma Duncan will go to get her story! But when
New Orleans' naughtiest boy, Damien Thorez,
lures this good girl into his world of steamy games
and forbidden temptations, she wonders if she's
crossed a line…or if she's really exposing her own
undercover fantasies.

1

In Gemma Duncan's fantasies, sweat would bead on her skin. It would trickle down her body to dampen the satin sheets while strangers—bad boys who never turned good—trailed their mouths over her belly.

They would dip their tongues into a navel pooled with summer heat, drag their kisses upward, over her writhing torso, her ribs, under the tender swell of her breast, drinking her in. They would never leave their names, but they *would* leave her tapped out physically, filled only with a surging need for more.

Gemma never talked about these fantasies.

But there were safer ones she would share with her new friends over happy-hour cocktails. Fantasies like winning a Pulitzer at the tender age of twenty-six. Fantasies where she would uncover nefarious activities of crime lords while crusading as a journalist at the New Orleans *Times-Picayunne*. Fantasies where she could bake a perfect soufflé, do a triple axle like Michelle Kwan and come home to a Garden District fantasy mansion full of fantasy puppies saved from the pound with her fantasy fortune.

As far as vivid imaginations went, she was number one. Hell, her fantasies even included knowing how to position a cell phone so that it always received perfect reception.

Needless to say, reality was a little different for Gemma Duncan.

"Jimmy?" she asked for the third time, walking five steps to the left and cocking her head to the right as she exited a French Quarter souvenir store. Taunting her, the phone fuzzed and stuttered in denial.

She'd had her older brother on the line only a second ago. "Jimmy? Can you hear me?"

The shop's zydeco music, with its energetic pulse of percussion and accordion, caused Gemma to plug one ear and wander through the muggy July air toward Dumaine Street. The threat of an afternoon rain braided itself with the smell of battered crawfish and spices from a nearby café.

"Hello?" She clutched her shopping bag, eager to talk to Jimmy and be back on her way to *The Weekly Gossip* offices in the Central Business District. Today she'd been interviewing a psychic who was integral to her latest deadline: Swamp Girl Finds Love with Tarot Reader.

Truly. That was it. This was why Gemma used a pen name—Duncan James—as opposed to her real one.

As she wandered farther down the street away from the tourists and toward her second destination, a voodoo shop, her older brother's voice squawked in and out of range.

Lunch-hour efficiency, she thought, somewhat proud of her scheduling skills. On Dumaine, she would not only achieve possible reception, but also buy a gris-gris bag of souvenirs for an out-of-town friend. Oh, and then there was that antique shop where she could see if that white-satin-gowned jazz-singer painting was still for sale....

"Jimmy," she said again, "I'm trying to... Ah, forget it. If you can hear me, I'm running errands anyway, so I bought that grotesque shellacked baby gator head for your wife. I'll send it priority mail tomorrow, okay? By the way, tell her happy birthday, you sicko. If *I* had a husband with a yen for weird gag gifts like you, there'd be some damage. And I say that with all the love in my heart. Talk to you later."

In one last hopeful attempt to achieve reception, Gemma paced near a courtyard. It had a wrought-iron gate and banana-tree leaves that leaned over the brick wall like a bored woman passing time while watching the street's infrequent traffic. Beyond the barriers, a man's raised voice competed with Jimmy's tinny bark.

"Gemma, I heard that. When you finally realize you've moved to the wrong city and listen to your family and move back here—"

Oops. "Not...understanding...a...word... you... say...." She snapped shut her cell phone, tucked it into the purse she'd slung crosswise over her chest and rested her spine against the courtyard bricks. She wiped at the heat steaming the straight tendrils of her upswept hair into curlicues while the man's disembodied voice continued to bluster behind the wall. A fountain tinkled in the background.

Water. The splashes reminded her of Orange County, California, where the dog days of summer were tempered by beach winds and swimming-pool afternoons.

But that's not where she belonged. She'd visited

New Orleans and had never left, especially after the *Weekly Gossip* job had come along. The tabloid had sounded good because she'd been desperate for income and experience.

Besides, the "Big Easy" had always sounded adventurous, a bit scary. Naughty.

The last place anyone who knew "nice" Gemma Duncan would've expected her to end up.

Over the courtyard wall, another male voice had joined the first one. Gemma idly closed her eyes, listening, lulled by the southern afternoon sounds.

"You're playing with some fire, here, Mr. Lamont. I'll leave now, before our meeting humiliates you further."

Gemma's eyes eased open, lured by the second man's voice. His tone had the rough undertow of a bayou night, where unknown dangers were hidden by darkness, the buzz of crickets, the lap of black water against crumbling docks.

A warm ache shocked her lower belly, then pulsed lower, urging her to press her thighs together. Man, if a mere voice could get her going, she really needed a date. Maybe it was time to start meeting more people and doing less work.

People such as…

She strained to hear him again—that echo of her fantasies: shadow-edged and wild, with just a hint of foreign danger.

Right, she thought. Only in my wildest dreams.

Most disappointingly, the first man was talking again, his N'awlins accent charged with anger. "You rigged that roulette wheel and bled me last night. Did you invite me to that gaming room with ruination in mind, Thorez?"

Thorez? She knew that name.

An intimidating pause spoke volumes, and she could imagine the accuser, Lamont, backing up a few steps.

"Anything else?" Thorez asked. "After all, you invited me to meet with you alone, and I expected to deal in some true business with a man of your stature. But your threats don't interest me, Lamont. Neither does your desperation."

"I resigned from the company three months ago, so you can't hold anything against me now." Lamont's voice shook a little. "I've become a better man."

"After you've tasted what your employees had to endure? I think so."

"What are you, Thorez? Some self-appointed avenger? Yes? I lost a lot of money in your joint. I could—"

"But you won't. You'll keep your voice down and go back to your home unruffled. Understand?"

Had Thorez stolen from this Lamont? And what was all this talk about employees and revenge?

Heart fluttering during the ensuing hesitation, Gemma shrank away from the gate, sheltering herself behind the brick wall. Maybe she should leave, but her inner journalist wouldn't allow it. Sometimes the best stories were the ones you stumbled over.

Damien Thorez was gossip gold, a city legend. A fixture in the Good Ol' Boy network.

Just by picturing what kind of man went with that kind of voice, she grew a little feverish.

Was he suave? Graying at the temples? As bearish as Tony Soprano?

While she considered it, Thorez's victim, Lamont,

was no doubt taking a moment to gather himself. He finally responded with more respect. "All I want is my money back, Mr. Thorez. I've worked hard for it."

"Not as hard as I did. And, rest assured, the proceeds will go to a proper place."

"Please!" Lamont's voice cracked. "I'll have to sell my home, you realize."

More silence cut through the humidity, and Gemma held her breath. The brick wall scratched against her cheek as she slipped down an inch, knee joints turning to liquid.

This was ridiculous, hiding like a child. Eavesdropping. But she couldn't leave. *Wouldn't* leave.

Heavy footsteps neared the gate. With a guilty start, Gemma opened her eyes, then darted behind a long, exhausted bronze Buick parked streetside. She held her crinkling plastic souvenir bag against her thigh, hoping it wouldn't make another sound.

She'd hit rock bottom, spying like this.

As the iron gate moaned open, Lamont's tortured voice echoed the rusty hinges. "You're not getting away with this. You are not all-powerful, Damien Thorez!"

Damien Thorez. Confirmation that this was the shady man she'd read about in the newspapers.

She could hear Thorez's steps come to a halt.

"I wish I had the power of gods," he said. "Then I'd fleece you in the afterlife, too, when we're both in hell."

Oh, what a quote *that*'d make. Gemma only wished she had her tiny recorder on.

From the sound of it, Lamont was getting braver, closer, as if he was at the gate, too. "Wouldn't the public love to know about these *other* dealings, sir?

Your weaknesses? I think a few of your competitors read the papers, if you catch my meaning."

Thorez merely laughed—but not because he was entertained, obviously. Or maybe he was.

By now, Gemma's head was swimming. This could lead to a real story. Maybe an exposé of one of New Orleans's most intriguing characters?

Her ticket to respect.

If she could just find out exactly what these "other" dealings were.

After the seemingly endless lack of response, Thorez spoke. "I think you're too smart to talk about my business, Mr. Lamont, if you catch *my* meaning."

That must have done the trick for the ex-CEO, be-causè Thorez continued swinging open the gate. He shut it with finality and walked away.

Oh, thank God, thank God, thank God he hadn't seen her crouched by the Buick.

As she waited a beat, a car drove by. Nonchalantly, Gemma flashed a smile at the miffed driver while he watched her hiding.

When he'd passed, she paused another moment, peeking around the car, watching an overweight, bald man—Lamont—as he trudged back toward his foliage-obscured brick home. Moments later, he slammed his door.

Quivering with the buzz of career success, Gemma peeked around the other side of the Buick, focusing on a tall, broad-shouldered, wiry figure as he moved down the street with the walk of a predator: slightly hunched, wary.

He had black shoulder-length hair that echoed the lazy wisps of a fine cigar's smoke. Hair that reminded her of a hallway in the dead of night when you have to drag a hand along the walls to find your way. A hallway where something might be waiting for you to pass, to feel the smile on its face when you discover it's there.

Was she going to pursue this? Damien Thorez wasn't a woman who lived in the sticks, professing to be a "swamp thing" in love with a psychic. He wasn't anyone else she usually wrote about, either—not the reincarnated Elvises or the women who claimed to be the next Marie Laveau.

Damien Thorez was her chance to make it big, to be taken seriously by everyone who'd expected more out of her than tabloid reporting. Even herself.

Hell, *yeah,* she was going to do this.

Gemma slyly removed herself from behind the Buick, trailing Thorez's panther stride, his black designer suit, the brightness of her future.

He rounded onto Royal Street, and she took care to act like a tourist, gawking at brightly hued buildings with their jolly paint-flaked shutters, the lacy iron fences, the stray drops from this morning's rain shower dripping on her head from galleries and balconies.

As Thorez moved onto St. Philip, the streets grew more deserted. Gemma wondered if she should stay on the beaten paths, if she'd entered an area where concierges warned their hotel guests to stay away from.

A hungover man without shoes told her in passing that he'd fallen asleep in front of a bar and someone had stolen his wallet and boots, and she just about turned right back to safer territory.

Brave Reporter Breaks Open The Truth About Notorious Criminal! screamed the headlines of her mind.

She kept going.

Finally, Thorez disappeared into a crumbling two-story wooden dwelling that squatted on a corner. The word *Cuffs* was painted in green over the awning-shrouded door.

Cuffs, huh? Gemma grinned, liking the place already. Her California-suburb family and friends would be shocked, but she was curious.

Not that she'd ever admit that out loud.

As she ventured closer, she wondered if this was Thorez's place. Everyone knew the man owned above-board businesses such as restaurants, bars and souvenir shops.

Ironically, he was said to own the exact store where she'd purchased the gator head today.

But she was more interested in *other* establishments—especially the ones Lamont had mentioned.

Gemma took a big breath, fortifying herself. She could barely even walk straight with all the adrenaline attacking her system.

When she finally made it inside, she didn't have long to absorb the murky atmosphere: the T-shirted, buzz-cut beefy men clutching the handles of mugs and watching a TV game show at the four-sided bar. The smell of booze and perspiration mixed by the slow blades of a ceiling fan. The clank of balls rolling over a pool table in the far corner.

Instead, a pair of strong arms engulfed her with the quickness of a flashing bite. One hand sprawled over her belly, pressing her back into a hard, lean body covered in linen. The other gripped her chin, turning her face toward her captor while he guided her into a deserted corner.

Thorez.

Only now, this close, could she see the feral glow of his pale blue eyes set against skin the color of a tobacco leaf.

Gemma tried to bite into his hand, but he loosened his hold while refusing to let go. Mouth quirked, his smile was mean, his gaze narrowed.

"It's not nice to follow people, *chère*."

Fear choked her throat, and she was painfully aware that her only weapon was a dime-store gator head wrapped in a plastic bag. Her heart jackhammered in her chest. He could feel her crazy pulse, couldn't he?

This wasn't a fantasy anymore.

Something shifted in his eyes, the shards of a broken kaleidoscope changing form, and he released her, except for the fingers that kept a hold of her skirt waistband.

God, she couldn't breathe. She couldn't run, either.

Yet, inexplicably, she took a step toward him.

His heavy eyebrow shot up. His half smile returned.

Her instinctive response had caught her unaware, also. But Gemma gathered all her courage and shed her old skin—the girl next door who'd made honor roll and the dean's list throughout school. The editor of every academic newspaper she'd worked on. Her family's great hope.

She shot a cheeky glance at his hand. His fingers had gone from grasping her waistband to settling on her hip, his thumb looped inside the skirt's rim.

Now that she could breathe again, she detected his scent: cool, mysterious, brandied.

"Do you mind?" she asked, directing her glance from his encroaching hand to his face.

"I mind being tailed, yeah," he said. "Is there something you want? My day's been full of demands."

Didn't she know it. "Your hand's still on me."

"So it is."

His smile widened, but it wasn't playful. No, this was what sin looked like when it was amused.

Gemma's blood rushed downward, making her stir uncomfortably. Making the inside of her thighs slick with the excitement of the chase. Making her swell and throb.

Dammit, she needed this story, and the enigmatic Damien Thorez was right here, ready for the unmasking.

She wasn't going to lose this chance.

Instead, she stilled the trembling in her lower stomach, hoping it wouldn't travel to her limbs.

It did.

But her voice was strong, even as she played dumb. "You own this place?"

He merely stared at her.

"I take that as a yes."

"Take it any way you want it."

Her appreciation for the art of a good double entendre tickled her nerves. Luckily, she found her steel again.

"I was wondering…" …*What you'd feel like against me…* "…if there were any openings. You know. For a waitress."

Genius, she thought. Working for him would be a good way to gather some sly information about these "other" dealings Lamont had hinted at.

But Thorez just continued staring.

"No?" she asked.

His thumb unhooked from her waistband, coasting lower, brushing over the center of her belly. Gemma jerked and grabbed his wrist as a bolt of desire shot through her. With emphatic meaning, she pushed his hand away.

"We're not hiring," he said. "For waitresses."

HARLEQUIN® *Temptation*®

AMERICAN HEROES

These men are heroes— strong, fearless... And impossible to resist!

Join bestselling authors Lori Foster, Donna Kauffman and Jill Shalvis as they deliver up

MEN OF COURAGE

Harlequin anthology
May 2003

Followed by *American Heroes* miniseries
in Harlequin Temptation

RILEY by Lori Foster
June 2003

SEAN by Donna Kauffman
July 2003

LUKE by Jill Shalvis
August 2003

Don't miss this sexy new miniseries by some of
Temptation's hottest authors!

Available at your favorite retail outlet.

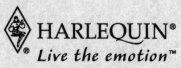

HARLEQUIN®
Live the emotion™

Visit us at www.eHarlequin.com

HTAH

It's hot...and out of control!

Don't miss these bold and ultrasexy books!

BUILDING A BAD BOY by Colleen Collins
Harlequin Temptation #1016
March 2005

WARM & WILLING by Kate Hoffmann
Harlequin Temptation #1017
April 2005

HER LAST TEMPTATION by Leslie Kelly
Harlequin Temptation #1028
June 2005

Look for these books at your favorite retail outlet.

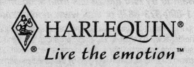

Live the emotion™

www.eHarlequin.com HTHEAT

If you enjoyed what you just read,
then we've got an offer you can't resist!

Take 2 bestselling love stories FREE!

Plus get a FREE surprise gift!

Clip this page and mail it to Harlequin Reader Service®

IN U.S.A.	IN CANADA
3010 Walden Ave.	P.O. Box 609
P.O. Box 1867	Fort Erie, Ontario
Buffalo, N.Y. 14240-1867	L2A 5X3

YES! Please send me 2 free Harlequin Temptation® novels and my free surprise gift. After receiving them, if I don't wish to receive anymore, I can return the shipping statement marked cancel. If I don't cancel, I will receive 4 brand-new novels each month, before they're available in stores. In the U.S.A., bill me at the bargain price of $3.80 plus 25¢ shipping and handling per book and applicable sales tax, if any*. In Canada, bill me at the bargain price of $4.47 plus 25¢ shipping and handling per book and applicable taxes**. That's the complete price and a savings of 10% off the cover prices—what a great deal! I understand that accepting the 2 free books and gift places me under no obligation ever to buy any books. I can always return a shipment and cancel at any time. Even if I never buy another book from Harlequin, the 2 free books and gift are mine to keep forever.

142 HDN DZ7U
342 HDN DZ7V

_____

Name   (PLEASE PRINT)

_____

Address   Apt.#

_____

City   State/Prov.   Zip/Postal Code

Not valid to current Harlequin Temptation® subscribers.

Want to try two free books from another series?
Call 1-800-873-8635 or visit www.morefreebooks.com.

* Terms and prices subject to change without notice. Sales tax applicable in N.Y.
** Canadian residents will be charged applicable provincial taxes and GST.
   All orders subject to approval. Offer limited to one per household.
   ® are registered trademarks owned and used by the trademark owner and its licensee.

TEMP04R   ©2004 Harlequin Enterprises Limited

◈ HARLEQUIN® *Blaze*™

The streets of New Orleans
are heating up with

BIG EASY
Bad Boys

Jeanie London

brings us an entire family of men with charm
and good looks to spare! You won't want
to miss Anthony DiLeo's story in

UNDER HIS SKIN
Harlequin Blaze #181
May 2005

Anthony is about to find out how an indecent proposal
fits into a simple business plan. When he approaches
Tess Hardaway with an idea to benefit both their companies,
she counters with an unexpected suggestion. A proposition
that involves the two of them getting to know each other
in the most intimate way!

Look for this book at your favorite retail outlet.

www.eHarlequin.com   HBBEBB0505

eHARLEQUIN.com
The Ultimate Destination for Women's Fiction

The ultimate destination for women's fiction.
Visit eHarlequin.com today!

GREAT BOOKS:
- We've got something for everyone—and at great low prices!
- Choose from new releases, backlist favorites, Themed Collections and preview upcoming books, too.
- Favorite authors: Debbie Macomber, Diana Palmer, Susan Wiggs and more!

EASY SHOPPING:
- Choose our convenient "bill me" option. No credit card required!
- Easy, secure, 24-hour shopping from the comfort of your own home.
- Sign-up for free membership and get $4 off your first purchase.
- Exclusive online offers: FREE books, bargain outlet savings, hot deals.

EXCLUSIVE FEATURES:
- Try Book Matcher—finding your favorite read has never been easier!
- Save & redeem Bonus Bucks.
- Another reason to love Fridays— Free Book Fridays!

Shop online
at www.eHarlequin.com today!

INTBB204

Brenda Jackson

and Silhouette Desire
present a hot new romance
starring another sexy
Westmoreland man!

JARED'S
COUNTERFEIT
FIANCÉE

(Silhouette Desire #1654)

When debonair attorney
Jared Westmoreland needed a date,
he immediately thought of the beautiful
Dana Rollins. Reluctantly, Dana fulfilled
his request, and the two were somehow
stuck pretending that they were engaged!
With the passion quickly rising between
them, would Jared's faux fiancée turn
into the real deal?

Available May 2005 at your favorite retail outlet.

Visit Silhouette Books at www.eHarlequin.com   SDJCF0405